THE
ARROW
COLLECTOR

THE
ARROW
COLLECTOR

CRISTIAN PERFUMO
TRANSLATED BY KEVIN GERRY DUNN

amazon crossing ◉

Text copyright © 2017 by Cristian Perfumo
Translation copyright © 2018 by Kevin Gerry Dunn
All rights reserved.

Previously published by author as *El coleccionista de flechas* in Spain in 2017. Translated from Spanish by Kevin Gerry Dunn. First published in English by AmazonCrossing in 2018.

Published by AmazonCrossing, Seattle

www.apub.com

Amazon, the Amazon logo, and AmazonCrossing are trademarks of Amazon.com, Inc., or its affiliates.

ISBN-13: 9781542040556
ISBN-10: 1542040558

Cover design by Kristen Haff

Printed in the United States of America

For you, dear reader.
Knowing you're on the other side of the page makes me
happy.

CHAPTER 1

"Here, look. Aim right for his heart," I instructed Manuel. "It should hit just to the side of his sternum."

I pressed my latex-gloved index finger into the bloodstained soccer jersey, feeling the soft give of the tall, muscular cop's Kevlar flak jacket beneath the fabric. He had been standing just like we told him for the past twenty minutes. Manuel made a minor adjustment, and the laser's red dot stopped at my fingertip.

"There, perfect. Don't move," I said. Then, turning to the cop, "You stay there, we almost have it." He nodded somberly.

"It's windy tonight. We need to do this at exactly the same time. I'll count to three and then you throw it. Ready?" Manuel said.

I took a small plastic tube from my pocket. "Ready."

"One, two, three."

I shook the tube in front of the cop, and a cloud of talcum powder revealed the red laser's path. I heard a burst of shots from Manuel's camera.

"Christ, warn us first!" cried Delia Echeverría, the judge, with an exaggerated, hoarse cough. The wind had blown the powder straight into her and the medical examiner's faces. The two had been talking a few steps behind the cop in the jersey.

"I think we got it with this one," Manuel said, showing me a photo. On the camera screen, the red laser drew a line from the iron gate we believed the attacker shot through straight to the cop's chest.

"Perfect," I agreed. "This clearly shows the shot had to come from behind the gate. The angle wouldn't make sense otherwise. The gate was probably closed, so they would have shot him from outside."

"What should I do now?" Manuel asked.

"Let's do it again, with him kneeling this time," I said, gesturing to the cop, who was wearing the jersey Norberto Pérez died in. The officer, who stood six feet tall, the same height as the victim, silently knelt facing us. "Luis says that according to the autopsy, the bullet entered through his chest but exited way lower, near his hips. He was probably on his knees and hit from above."

After another fifteen minutes of talcum powder and photographs, we finished reconstructing the scene and started packing up our equipment. Heads poked out from the windows of nearby houses, only to withdraw when they saw *CSI UNIT* printed on the back of our jackets.

"What're you doing after this?" Manuel asked, folding the tripod he had mounted the laser on.

"Going back to the courthouse to do the write-up."

"But it's ten at night."

"It has to be ready tomorrow," I said quietly, gesturing toward Judge Echeverría, who was talking to the medical examiner about which organs the gunshot had ripped through.

"You're going to spend all night writing the report?"

"I mean, if it takes all night, then yeah."

"I'll tell you what. How about I help with the report, and then if it's not too late when we finish, we go get a drink. Deal?" He stuck out a hand for me to shake. He was still wearing the blue latex gloves.

"Thanks, but I'm exhausted. All I'll want to do when I finish the report is go to bed."

I briefly considered whether I'd been too hard on Manuel. He was such a good guy, always willing to help out. But I just wasn't attracted to him at all. I was trying to convey this in the nicest way possible.

Fortunately, I was interrupted by my phone vibrating in my pocket. "Hello?"

"Officer Badía, this is Sergeant Debarnot. Are you available?"

"I'm doing the laser analysis for the Pérez case. We're just wrapping up. Did something happen?"

"A homicide on Estrada Street. I just arrived at the house and confirmed it. Male, around forty."

"Don't touch anything. I'm on my way. What's the street number?"

"Fourteen twenty-three. Across from Antonio Oneto Elementary School."

A tight knot formed in my stomach. "Is it a big stone house?"

"Yes."

"Shit."

"What is it?" Debarnot asked on the other end of the line.

"I . . . nothing. Did the victim have short black hair? A little gray?"

"Yes. I'm almost certain it's the owner of Impekable, that cleaning supply store. Do you want me to check his pockets for some sort of identification?"

"No, don't touch anything. I'm heading over."

I didn't need him to ID the victim. I knew perfectly well that it was Julio Ortega. I knew this because we dated when I was in high school, and because two months earlier, we spent the night together in the house where he had just been found dead.

CHAPTER 2

Outside the stone house on Estrada Street, Commissioner Lamuedra's personal vehicle was parked between two squad cars.

I greeted the two officers standing guard outside. One of them, plump and not in uniform, was Debarnot. I went in and looked around.

"Laura, how's it going?" Lamuedra greeted me with a kiss on the cheek.

"I'm fine, Commissioner, how are you?"

"I'm . . . it's after ten at night and they're making me work. I could be better. The body's in the dining room. Follow me. And watch your step."

Too late. Before Lamuedra finished speaking, I heard a crunch under my foot, which had landed on a pile of broken glass beneath the front hall window. Beside it was a plastic-bristled broom that the police must have used to gather up the shards.

"Who swept this up? Debarnot, I told you on the phone to make sure no one touches anything. We could end up losing fingerprints."

"The broom was there when the body was found. No one touched anything . . . or, at least, they hadn't," he added, looking at my foot.

I pointed to the hall window, which was covered by a thick red curtain. "Did the intruder come in through there?"

Lamuedra shook his head and pulled away the curtain. The shutters were closed and the glass was intact.

"Where did all this glass come from, then?"

Lamuedra shrugged. "You're the CSI," he responded, gesturing with his head for me to follow him farther into the house.

The hallway to the dining room had been redecorated since my visit two months earlier. The photos of Julio with his girlfriend—by the glacier, in Búzios, at the waterfalls—no longer hung on the walls. There were still two of Julio alone in Buenos Aires, though: one in front of the Obelisk and another at River Plate Stadium.

The police had turned on all the lights in the dining room. People always expect crime scenes to be dark like they are in the movies, but in real life, we illuminate them as much as possible, to help us understand the story that the corpse and the objects around it tell. I didn't see any corpse, though, just furniture: an oval table and six hardwood chairs, a beige sofa with its back to the rest of the room, facing the enormous TV on the wall.

Commissioner Lamuedra motioned for me to follow him around the sofa. As we approached, I saw two feet in beige boat shoes, then a pair of navy pants, a white shirt, and finally, Julio's head. His eyes were open, and his face was disfigured from being badly beaten. The body lay on its left side, in the fetal position, hands tucked between the knees. He had probably taken that position instinctively, to minimize the pain and protect his vital organs.

"Who found him?" I asked, looking away.

"Debarnot, by accident," Lamuedra said, pointing to the front door with his thumb. "He wasn't on duty. He was driving past and thought it was weird for the front door to be open when it's so cold and windy out. He stopped and waited a few minutes, and then went in when he didn't see any movement inside."

"And he didn't touch anything?"

Lamuedra sighed. "No, Laura, he didn't touch anything."

I knelt in a corner of the room, opened the kit I'd brought with me, put on a pair of latex gloves, and took several deep breaths, pretending to slowly contemplate the scene. Then, mustering my courage, I crouched beside the corpse of my high school boyfriend and recent one-night stand.

His face was covered in cuts and bruises, like a boxer after a match. When I lifted his upper lip, I saw he was missing his two front teeth. His white shirt was stained with thick red streaks where fat drops of blood had rolled down his chest, along with the more diffuse bursts of droplets that would have followed every blow.

His hands were fully coated in red. When I examined them, I saw that there was a small, circular wound on the back of each. With so much blood, it was impossible to determine the cause. I trusted that the medical examiner would be able to explain it after the autopsy.

I grabbed my camera and took close-ups of the body from several angles, as well as shots of the face and hands. Then I took several from farther back, to capture the entire scene.

Behind the sofa, next to the oval table, an enormous antique wardrobe held a collection of tumblers and wine glasses. All still intact. I inspected every window in the house, but I was unable to determine the origin of the swept-up shards in the front hall.

"There's more blood over here," Debarnot shouted from the hallway.

I found him crouching on the floor, pointing one of his pudgy fingers at a small red-brown stain near the baseboard. The circular pattern surrounded by smaller stains suggested the blood had dripped from fairly high. Considering how far we were from the body, I figured it fell from the attacker's bloody hands as he fled. Or maybe Julio, trying to defend himself, had managed to inflict his killer with a small wound.

I took several photos of the drop and then dabbed at it with a cotton swab. It was completely dry. I scraped at it with the blade of a knife and collected the brown flakes into a tube for lab analysis. We scanned the rest of the house inch by inch, but we didn't find any more blood.

I took a few more photos of the corpse and gave the order to have the body transferred to the morgue. While we waited, I returned to the broken glass near the front door, beneath the intact window. I took some plastic freezer bags from my kit and placed the shards in them, one by one. I counted over fifty.

The only piece of furniture in the tiny front hall was a corner cabinet with a glass door, also untouched. I crouched down to make sure no glass had slid beneath it. And, lo and behold, when I shined my flashlight, something sparkled back at me.

I felt around with my gloved hand until I touched an object that was too irregular to be a piece of glass. When I placed it in the palm of my hand, I saw that it was an arrowhead, about two inches long.

It was a beautiful, teardrop-shaped piece. When I held it under the light, it reflected iridescent rays, like the inside of a mussel shell. I'd never seen an arrowhead do that. The Tehuelches, the native people from this part of Patagonia, made arrowheads that were ochre, yellow, black, white, green—even transparent. But I had never seen one that was iridescent like that.

CHAPTER 3

When I got to the courthouse the next day, I dropped my coat off in my lab, then hurried to the second floor, taking the stairs two at a time. I turned right and there she was, just like every other morning: Isabel Moreno, her eyes glued to her phone.

"You're late," she said with a smile.

"Am I? I didn't realize."

"Everyone else is already inside."

She pointed to the wood door of the judge's chambers with one of her exceedingly long fuchsia fingernails.

"Just a second. Where do you think you're going?" she said to my back, raising her voice.

"Isn't it obvious? There is a meeting about a case. I have to be in that meeting. I am going to that meeting. Do you need me to make you a flowchart?"

"But you can't just go *in*. I have to announce you first. There's a reason the judge has a secretary."

And that's what it was like every fucking time I talked to Isabel Moreno. I always thought of her as "the Harpy," though I never felt particularly moved to share that nickname with anyone. She was a fortysomething woman who had been a court administrator for over twenty years. In fact, she'd been there longer than anyone. And the way she saw it, her seniority gave her privileges that weren't spelled out in her job description.

"You don't need to announce me. They're waiting," I said.

"So now you're telling me how to do my job?"

The fact that a man left her for me two years earlier hadn't done wonders for our relationship, either.

"For fuck's sake, Isabel, it's too early for this," I said, opening the door.

◆ ◆ ◆

"Finally!" exclaimed Echeverría, looking up from some papers.

"Good morning, everybody, sorry to keep you waiting," I said, forcing a smile for the judge and the two men sitting across her desk: Commissioner Lamuedra on the left and Sergeant Debarnot, the guy who'd found Julio Ortega's body, on the right.

A large window gave Judge Echeverría an incredible view of the estuary, which shifted between gray and turquoise, depending on the sky, the wind, and the tide. That morning, the water was a deep blue, and it was moving forcefully to the west with the rising tide.

Across the estuary, the completely uninhabited south bank extended toward the horizon. The only building on that side was an abandoned house from another era. People say it used to belong to a fisherman. Half a mile to the west, an enormous Y-shaped volcanic stone a British explorer had dubbed "Tower Rock" stood in defiance of gravity.

When Lamuedra saw there were no more chairs, he gestured for me to take his. I insisted that it wouldn't be necessary and sat on a big iron safe next to the window, beneath a large painting.

"Sergeant Debarnot was just starting to tell us how he found the body. Start from the beginning so that Detective Badía will be caught up," Echeverría said.

Debarnot nodded somberly.

"Yesterday, I was tasked with a foot patrol through the old part of town with First Corporal Vilchez."

"Where Ortega's house is."

"That's correct. We began our patrol at quarter past four in the afternoon. At approximately four thirty, we passed Ortega's house and observed that the door was open. I recall that detail clearly because we made several jokes about how cold the interior of the house must be."

He wasn't even thirty, but Debarnot always talked with the unwavering seriousness of an old-time cop. He hadn't learned that jargon at the police academy; he'd learned it in his own home. His father, Flaco Debarnot, had been commissioner in the eighties, and the police in Puerto Deseado still talked about his sense of justice and his fearlessness.

"And it didn't occur to you to see if everything was okay?" asked Lamuedra. "In half an hour it was going to be totally dark. You didn't think it was suspicious for someone to leave their front door open in the middle of winter?"

"No sir, the truth is we didn't think about it."

"If you had just knocked . . ." Lamuedra started, but Echeverría gestured for him to hush.

"You can't blame me for that, Commissioner."

If any other sub-officer had talked back like that, there would've been hell to pay. But Mariano Debarnot enjoyed a privileged position within the precinct. The Debarnot name allowed him to move comfortably on both sides of the not-so-invisible veil that separates the officers from the non-coms on any police force.

"Continue, please," intervened Echeverría.

"Last night, when my shift was over, I went to play soccer. Several of us at the station have formed a team, and we're participating in a tournament. After the game, I drove by Ortega's house. I guess that on some level, the door being open must have struck me as odd, because I went back."

"And it was still open," I ventured.

"Correct. It had now been dark for five hours. Given the cold last night, I thought that surely something unusual had happened."

"What time was this?"

"The game concluded at ten, so this would have been at ten twenty. I parked in front of the house and knocked repeatedly before entering."

Debarnot took a breath before continuing. His voice was firm and his expression was hard. He seemed to be concentrating on showing the commissioner and the judge that he was brave, and that the awful scene he'd walked in on hadn't affected him.

"When I entered the residence, I found Ortega's body."

"And that was when you called the station?"

"Correct. Immediately after checking his pulse and confirming he was deceased."

"And you searched the rest of the house?"

"No, I didn't have my service weapon with me. The attacker could have still been there."

"We now know that wasn't the case," I added. "Didn't you say the door had been open since at least five o'clock? And anyway, the blood had been coagulated for several hours."

Echeverría stepped in: "That's easy to say now, but Sergeant Debarnot was unaware of it at the time."

Debarnot kept talking, apparently not noticing that Echeverría had thrown him a line. I wasn't sure if he was trying to play it cool to help me save face with the judge or if he was trying not to admit he'd been afraid to search the house.

"You know the rest. Ten minutes later, you two were in that dining room with me."

CHAPTER 4

Judge Echeverría thanked Debarnot, and Commissioner Lamuedra told him to get back to work. When it was just the three of us in her chambers, Echeverría kept her eyes on Lamuedra as she spoke to me.

"The commissioner and I would like you to handle this case, Laura."

"Of course. I'm heading to the lab now to analyze the evidence."

"I don't mean like that. Or at least, not *only* like that."

"I don't understand," I said, though I understood perfectly.

"We want you to wear both of your hats for this one. You'll be our forensic detective when you're analyzing evidence, and a police officer when you're taking statements from witnesses, talking to the neighbors, those sorts of things."

"But I haven't done police work in almost three years."

Lamuedra huffed. "Do I really need to remind you that you're a cop? You're only on loan to the court forensics lab." He felt the need to repeat himself: "On *loan.*"

Echeverría stepped in: "Laura, why did you agree to work at the court three years ago?"

I looked at her. I was floored. She knew perfectly well why.

"Because here I can spend the bulk of my time doing forensic work. On the police force, even when we're in the middle of a homicide investigation, there are always a million other things to take care of, and they all bore me to tears: patrols, watches, security operations. None of it has anything to do with solving crimes, and honestly, I couldn't care less about any of it. I think I'm more useful working for the court than I am on the police force."

I expected Lamuedra to have some kind of reaction, but he just listened calmly, then nodded at Echeverría, signaling for her to say whatever she was about to say.

"Laura," she said, "your loan agreement expires in less than a year. And seeing as the commissioner and I also believe your skills are best suited for the court, we would like to offer you a permanent transfer. Which would practically guarantee you the forensic detective job for life."

"We could make it official once you close this case," added Lamuedra.

I smiled as I processed this news. If I didn't know Echeverría and Lamuedra so well, I'd have taken this as an incentive to accept the case. But all three of us knew perfectly well that an incentive wasn't necessary. They were my bosses. I had to follow their orders, end of story.

They weren't offering me the transfer in exchange for accepting the case. In fact, it was just the opposite: if I gave them any trouble, I could forget about my transfer.

"You're the best we've got in the precinct right now," Lamuedra added, patting my shoulder.

My first thought was to come up with some kind of excuse. A lie that made clear I didn't need to be the one heading up this case. But it would raise red flags if any officer chose to forgo a chance like this—and that went double for me. If I wanted to get out of it, I'd have to tell them the truth: I'd slept with the victim two months ago. Needless to say, that was a conflict of interest as big as Brazil. And then they'd remove me from the investigation completely, as both a cop and a CSI.

But I wasn't so sure I wanted out. Did I really want to watch what promised to be the most interesting case in years from the sidelines? Not to mention the chance of a permanent transfer to the court, where my work felt ten times more relevant than it did on the force.

"And anyway," added Lamuedra, "everyone's favorite asshole, Ruiz, broke his ankle and fibula playing soccer, and Inspector Peláez is on maternity leave."

"Nice to know you turn to me when you have no other choice."

"Doesn't anything make you happy?" snapped Lamuedra. "If I ask you to do police work, you get pissy, and if I don't ask you to do police work, you still get pissy."

There was a knock on the door before I could respond. It was Manuel Locane, from the court's technical team. The same guy who'd wanted to get a drink with me the night before. He greeted us with a silent wave and took the seat Debarnot had been sitting in five minutes earlier.

"Locane, Detective Badía will be leading the investigation," said Judge Echeverría with finality. "What do we know about the victim?"

"All I could do between last night and this morning was research him online," said Manuel, opening a laptop on the desk. "Mainly on social media. We'll have to confirm and get more info through interviews."

He ran a hand over his shaved head, pushing imaginary hair off his face, and started typing at the speed of light.

"Julio Ortega: Argentinian, forty-three years old. Owner of Impekable, the cleaning supply store on Sarmiento Street. It looks like lately things weren't going so well, because on Facebook he posted dozens of offers to sell it off."

"Unmarried?" asked Lamuedra.

"Yes. According to his Facebook profile, he's been in a relationship with a woman named Noelia Guillón for years."

"And you already notified the girlfriend?" I asked, turning away from my colleagues, pretending to study the canvas above the safe.

The painting depicted a bar where all of the customers were numbers with little arms and legs. My favorite was an eight wearing a sombrero and leaning against the bar with a shot of tequila. Ever since the day I'd overheard a conversation I shouldn't have, whenever I looked at that painting, I wondered what those numbers had to do with the combination to the safe beneath them.

"No, because she's not family," said Echeverría. "If she were his wife, it would be different."

"She's apparently on vacation," said Manuel. "For the past three days she's been posting photos from Iguazú Falls nonstop."

"Who else is in the photos?" asked Lamuedra.

"She's alone."

"Well, Detective Badía can be in charge of notifying her."

"But she's not family," I said, echoing Echeverría.

"That just means we're not required to tell her," said Lamuedra. "But we can still apply a little common sense. It's better she hears it from us than some other way. Don't you agree, Your Honor?"

"I do," said Echeverría. "Tell her, Laura."

I nodded three times, thinking the same word with each movement of my head: *shit, shit, shit.*

"So, what family members know Ortega's dead?" asked Lamuedra.

"We were unable to find direct relatives," responded Echeverría. "We put an ad about it on the radio. I'm sure they'll start broadcasting it this morning."

"His parents died when he was young," I chimed in.

"How do you know *that*?" she said.

"When I was in high school, Ortega was kind of the town sex symbol. The twentysomething rebel all the teenage girls fantasized about. And in a town this small, most of his admirers knew his biography pretty well."

"And *you* were one of those admirers?" asked Manuel.

"Badía, tell us what else you know about Ortega," interjected Lamuedra.

"Not much," I answered. My stomach tightened. I was withholding information from my direct superiors. It wouldn't be a big deal if they found out about a fleeting romance when I was a teenager, but if they learned about what happened two months ago . . .

"It seems like he had a taste for the finer things," said Manuel, interrupting my thoughts. "He posted a lot of photos of imported beers and whiskey. He was fond of gambling, too. On his profile there were screenshots of his score on different gambling apps and photos of him posing in front of all the casinos he visited. The ones in Mar del Plata, Puerto Madero, Comodoro Rivadavia, Puerto Madryn, and obviously, Puerto Deseado."

"That's a good place to start, especially if his gambling was pathological. Badía, I want you to find out if Ortega owed anyone money," said Lamuedra.

I nodded, a little taken aback. It didn't surprise me that Julio had a hedonistic streak, but I had no idea about the gambling.

"Anything else?" asked Echeverría, looking at the three of us.

"I can't make sense of the broom and broken glass in the front hall," I said. "None of the glass things in the house were broken. Where could they have come from?"

"It might not be related to the case. Maybe something broke and Ortega was sweeping it up when he was attacked," said Lamuedra.

"Sure, but what would have broken? Where did all of those shards come from? The arrowhead I found under the cabinet is also weird."

"If you think it's relevant, investigate it. Like I said, Laura, you're in charge," said Echeverría, bringing the meeting to a close.

The first thing I did when I stepped out of the judge's chambers was open Facebook on my phone and unfriend Julio Ortega. The second thing I did was find Debarnot and put him charge of telling the girlfriend about the murder. I made up something about how since he had been the one to find the body, it was only logical he should tell her. He tried to convince me otherwise, but I insisted and eventually he gave in, though he gave me some attitude about it.

Under different circumstances, I would have put him in his place. Like the time I told Corporal Ramírez that if he had a problem taking orders from a woman, I'd be glad to buy him a ticket back to the nineteenth century. But I couldn't come up with anything half that clever for Debarnot right then.

I just wanted to make damn sure I wasn't the one breaking the news to Julio's girlfriend.

CHAPTER 5

The door to my lab in the courthouse opened so suddenly that I dropped the piece of glass I was holding, which broke in two on the stainless steel table. It was Manuel.

"Jesus, Manuel, can you knock?"

"Sorry, I just . . ." His words trailed off when he saw what I'd been working on for the past hour. "You must be good at jigsaw puzzles."

After using powder to lift the fingerprints, I'd laid all the shards of glass out on the table—there were fifty-three in the end—and reconstructed a twenty-by-fifteen-inch rectangle. I'd started with the edges, like you do with real puzzles, and now I was at the hard part: figuring out where the middle pieces went. But that was less important. The critical thing had been figuring out the original dimensions of the glass.

"Looks like you got some prints," said Manuel, pointing to the shards of glass covered in black powder.

"Yeah, there were a few. Most are Ortega's, but there are some others. Like these four on one of the sides," I said, showing him the transparent rectangles that the adhesive tape had left when I lifted the prints from the black powder.

"Have you figured out where the glass came from?"

"I've got some theories, but nothing concrete."

"Really? Theories, wow, that's really cool. Me, I don't even have any theories." A closed-lip smirk spread across his face. "I do have an answer, though." He reached into the pocket of his jeans and pulled out Julio's phone, which I'd given him to analyze. "Now look me in the eye and tell me I don't deserve to take you out some night. It's sixty-nine, sixty-nine, baby."

"What?"

"That's the new code I put on the phone."

"You're a moron, you know that? Tell me you found something that makes it worth putting up with you."

"Of course. If I hadn't, I wouldn't be here bothering you, Detective Badía."

Manuel entered the code and pulled up a photo of a display case in which several arrowheads were affixed to a red velvet backing. I'd seen lots of collections just like this: Patagonia was full of hobbyists who searched for Tehuelche arrowheads, and this kind of case was their preferred way of displaying them.

Twelve arrowheads were arranged in a triangle, with a wider thirteenth in the center. I zoomed in and looked at the pieces one by one. They all had the same teardrop shape and iridescence as the one I'd found at the crime scene.

A reflection in a corner of the case showed that they were protected under a pane of glass, which I estimated to have the same dimensions as the rectangle I was in the process of reconstructing.

"We have to show this to the judge," I said.

"Too late. I already showed her."

"What did she say?"

"She's going to send the photo to an archaeologist friend in Buenos Aires, though I don't think anything'll come of it."

"Yeah, seems like kind of a long shot," I said.

I couldn't have been more wrong.

CHAPTER 6

The next day, it was so cold outside that it felt cozy inside the morgue.

The building where all of the town's autopsies were conducted looked like a garage more than anything else. It was even the right size. And if you didn't know what the space was used for and went inside, it would just look like a storeroom for old boxes, with a strange stainless steel bathtub in the middle and an oversized freezer in the corner.

Luis Guerra, Puerto Deseado's medical examiner, was sitting in a chair with his feet up on the autopsy table. His glasses were balanced on the end of his nose, and he was using his index finger to jab at the smartphone his daughter had just given him for his fifty-fifth birthday. On the floor next to him was his constant companion, a hot cup of coffee.

"Laura, finally. I was about to start without you." He had been in Puerto Deseado for twenty years, and his Córdoba accent was as strong as ever.

"You said eight o'clock. It's ten till. And, please, don't feel like you have to get up to greet me or anything. I'll just crouch down to your level."

He laughed, grabbed his coffee, and stood up to give me a quick kiss on the cheek.

"Do you want a coffee?"

"I'm good, thank you," I said, hanging my things on the coatrack. I opened a cabinet and put on a pair of latex gloves. "Could we get started right away? Today's going to be long."

"Whatever you say. After all, I'm the medical examiner and you're my assistant. You say 'jump' and I say 'how high?'"

"You're damn straight you do, if you want your assistant to stick around," I retorted, smiling.

It was true, I didn't have to be there for autopsies, but I went because it made things easier for Luis, and because I learned a ton of things that ended up helping me understand murder scenes. And Luis was an incredible teacher.

"Which one's he in?" I asked, gesturing toward the four freezer doors.

Luis put on his gloves and walked around the dissection table. He grabbed the handle of one of the doors and pulled, taking two steps back as he did. The seven-foot aluminum tray slid out until Julio's entire body was exposed.

When I saw him, I felt a stab in my stomach, like the first time I went to a morgue. But that was fifteen years ago, and I hadn't felt that way since: not as a cop, not as a forensics student, and not at any other point in my career. Corpses had become a tool I used for my job.

But this wasn't just another corpse.

Luis took the grips at the head of the tray. I took the ones by the feet.

"One, two, three," he said. We lifted the body and carried it to the autopsy table.

Julio was still covered in blood and still wearing the clothes he'd died in. Luis removed the boat shoes and socks, then took a pair of scissors from one of the shelves behind him and started cutting off the pants. I did the same with the bloodstained white shirt.

Once the clothes were off, Luis turned on the water and we began washing the body. It took at least ten minutes to get all the dried blood off Julio's face, hair, neck, and hands. When we finished, Luis pointed to his phone, which he'd left on a rack on the other side of the room, next to his coffee.

"See if that thing has a voice recorder, like yours."

"They all do."

"Then take off your gloves and start recording so we can begin. I'm sick of using that piece of crap that always snags on the tape," he said, gesturing toward a cassette recorder as old as me that, until that very day, Luis had been using to keep his autopsy logs.

I downloaded a voice memo app, started recording, and placed the phone on the table, about three inches from the corpse's short hair, which was still wet.

"This is medical examiner Luis Guerra, assisted by Detective Laura Badía. We are beginning the autopsy of Julio Ortega at 8:24 a.m. on August 9, 2017, at the morgue of the Court of First Instance of Puerto Deseado, Santa Cruz Province, Argentina. The cadaver bears multiple lacerations and hematomas on the face and head, the result of blunt force trauma, most likely from fists."

Luis's gaze moved slowly down Julio's body, pausing at the stomach.

"There are also hematomas in the abdominal zone, some extending to the sternum and the lower thorax."

He pushed into the stomach and lifted the arms to look underneath. He paused at the back of one of the hands. After pushing his glasses back on his nose with his own wrist, he looked at it more closely.

"I noticed those marks when I examined the body the night we found it. What are they?" I asked, putting on a new pair of gloves.

"Circular lesions. But they're old. Look, they were already scarring. They look like burns."

"Like someone put out a cigarette on his skin," I said, picking up the hand to examine it. When I touched the cadaver, the nauseous feeling rushed back to my stomach, and I let go.

Clunk. Julio's knuckles landed on the stainless steel.

"They're not from a cigarette," Luis said with certainty. "They're too deep. A cigarette would have gone out before penetrating the epidermis."

"What are they from, then?"

"I'd say a blowtorch or a hot metal object, but we'll have a better idea when we look at the tissue under the microscope."

"How long has he had them? A week?"

"Maybe a little longer. Looking at the tissue will help clear that up, too. But let's start with the macro stuff. There'll be time for the micro stuff later."

Luis turned to a shelf and opened a drawer the size of a paperback novel. When he turned back around, he was holding his scalpel in one hand and my knife in the other.

I'd had it made by a craftsman in Buenos Aires when I was starting to do autopsies as part of my degree. Most of my classmates preferred scalpels, but a knife always felt more comfortable in my hand. And safer, because I'd designed the handle with a little shield where the wood joined the blade, to keep me from inadvertently slicing off a finger.

"Is opening him necessary?" I asked.

"Well, yes . . . it's an autopsy," he answered, taken aback. "We don't know if the cause of death was from blows to the head or to the abdomen. Or another thing altogether. If nothing else, we have to see if there was any internal hemorrhaging."

I nodded silently. For an instant, I wondered what difference it made which exact blows he'd died from. He'd been beaten to death, and anyone else would tell you that was all that really mattered.

I closed my eyes and took a deep breath. I was horrified to catch myself thinking like that, like "anyone else." As if I didn't understand the relevance a detail like that could have in a trial.

"Do you want to make the incision?" Luis asked, offering the knife to me over the corpse.

"Sure," I lied.

"Then take your knife?"

"Yes, sorry, of course."

I took another deep breath and looked at the stainless steel blade streaked from countless runs against the sharpening stone. The powerful light above us bounced off the blade and onto the lifeless body. The reflection jumped around as my hand trembled.

"What's wrong?"

"I don't know. I don't feel good."

"Well, don't go vomiting and making a mess of all our work."

He was smiling, but his expression froze when he made eye contact. "Laura, you're pale. Should we step outside for a minute?"

I shook my head.

"Do you want to go home? I can do this myself."

I shook my head harder and pressed the edge of my knife against Julio's bruised sternum. All I had to do was push and slide the blade back, like I'd done dozens of times before.

What the fuck is wrong with you, Laura? I thought. *You're fine. Take a deep breath, then do it.*

I sucked in my breath and held it. Looking at Julio's naked, discolored body, I remembered when I was sixteen and kissed him for the first time, outside the high school. I remembered the corny love letters he used to write me, even though I was totally the one who was infatuated with him, and how I could never think of anything genuine to say when I sat down to write back—I'd wanted to be with him because Julio Ortega was everyone's crush back then, but it turns out there wasn't much substance behind my infatuation. I remembered the day I decided I felt nothing for him and told him so. And I remembered our chance encounter, barely two months ago, after so many years. I exhaled heavily, letting out all my breath at once.

"Sorry, Luis, I can't."

I walked to the door quickly, leaving my knife on a chest that I had caressed only two months earlier.

CHAPTER 7

I stood naked in my bathroom. I'd undressed like an automaton, unthinking. My head was still at the morgue, where twenty minutes ago, for the first time in my life, I'd frozen when faced with a cadaver.

I spent a second looking at the two thick red streaks on the shower curtain. They were in the unmistakable shape of two bloody hands clutching at the plastic before falling to the ground.

Maybe it's time to get a new shower curtain, I thought as I ran the water. I briefly fantasized about moving to the mountains and earning a living doing literally anything else. It was something that had been crossing my mind more and more recently, even though it wasn't something I'd ever consider actually doing.

When the shower was hot enough, I stepped into the tub, closed my eyes, and stuck my head directly under the running water. I don't know how long I stood there, not moving, letting the water pound at my face as I tried, unsuccessfully, to stop thinking. The image of Julio's body was etched in my retinas.

I had never failed to perform an autopsy before. Not even when we were working on the bony, fair-skinned corpse of Miss Cristina, my first-grade teacher, or the bloated body of Daniela, my childhood neighbor, who I used to play with outside when it wasn't too cold.

It's not like I was some kind of unfeeling monster, either. I was devastated when I heard Daniela had drowned in the estuary, leaving her two babies without a mother. I even cried right before entering the morgue. But once I was inside, I did my job as usual. In the end, the body wasn't the person I had known; it was simply a mass of tissue that Luis and I methodically and precisely dissected in order to get the answers we needed.

Until today, I had always managed to check my emotions at the door.

It was an important job, but not many people could stomach it.

And virtually no one understood it.

It's not always pleasant, but I love it, I thought as I lathered the shampoo into my hair. I smiled, a little surprised to catch myself thinking the same line I'd used a thousand times to defend myself when people confessed (unprompted) that they could never do what I do.

Things would've been very different if I'd stayed in Buenos Aires after getting my degree. *That* would have made my job unbearable. All my friends there spent years specializing in one specific area of work. The one who chose ballistics spent five days a week analyzing projectiles. The one who chose fingerprints did fingerprints. But since I was the only forensics expert in town, I got to do a little bit of everything. Sometimes I analyzed car break-ins, sometimes I photographed bloodstains, and every once in a while, I helped Luis with an autopsy, which he always turned into a master class.

Of course I was passionate about what I did. Otherwise, I wouldn't have set my phone to play a gunshot sound effect whenever I got a text. And I wouldn't have asked my aunt's painting instructor to draw what looked like the marks of two bloody hands on my shower curtain.

Today was a fluke, I concluded. It could have happened to anyone. It was certainly no reason to run off to the mountains.

CHAPTER 8

I had just finished soaping up when the shower started losing pressure.

No, no, no, I thought, hurrying to rinse myself off under the withering stream, which would reduce to a drip in a matter of seconds.

"Shit," I said out loud, forcefully sweeping aside the shower curtain.

It was the third time that month I'd run out of water. It turns out I was jealous of my friends in Buenos Aires after all: they might spend their days analyzing fingerprints, but they also got to shower without any surprises.

One of them had visited me a few years earlier, and she couldn't get it through her head that Puerto Deseado only got running water for a few hours every four days. Everyone fills their household tanks, and then they have to make that last until the next time we get water. When I told her lots of people wake up before dawn to turn on their washing machines, because that's when the water is on, she roared with laughter, thinking I was joking.

I tried to towel the suds out of my hair and off my legs and back.

Then I heard the gunshot in the living room. Someone had texted me. I wrapped myself in the towel and went to look for my phone.

I had two missed calls from the judge. She had also sent the text, which said I should call right away. She picked up before the second ring.

"Laura, forgive me for being so insistent. Is this a good time to talk?"

"Sure," I lied. "Should I come to the courthouse?"

"No, there's no need. It's important, but I can tell you over the phone. I just spoke to an archaeologist friend of mine in Buenos Aires. A leading figure in Tehuelche studies."

"The one you asked to look at the photo we found on Ortega's phone?"

"Precisely. You're going to like this. It turns out that it's a very special collection, and apparently people would pay good money for those arrowheads on the black market. Private collectors obsessed with owning something no one else can have. You know, eccentrics."

"How much are they worth?"

"At first Alberto didn't want to hazard a figure. He said it was 'very difficult to appraise something that is simultaneously a piece of world heritage, a historical touchstone, and a specimen of crucial importance to scholars across the globe,'" she quoted in a tone of faux male solemnity, "but I pressed him a little and he said if he had to put a price tag on it, it would be around fifty thousand US dollars."

"So the arrowheads could have been the motive for the homicide."

"It's at least something to consider. The assailant might have been in a hurry to get away from the scene and could have smashed the case unintentionally, which would explain the shards of glass and the arrowhead you found."

"It would," I said, "but someone swept up the shards."

"You're right, that doesn't fit. Even so, given how much the arrowheads are worth, it seems like the robbery angle deserves more attention. Wouldn't you agree?"

"Definitely. Could you give me your friend's number? I'd like to ask him some questions."

"There's no need. He'll be in Puerto Deseado tomorrow."

"Seriously? He's coming all the way from Buenos Aires?"

"Laura, he's an archaeology scholar. His life isn't exactly a thrill a minute."

I laughed and felt the tightness of dry soap suds on my cheeks.

After saying goodbye to Echeverría, I went to my room and stuffed a change of clothes into a bag. I'd have to finish showering at my aunt's house.

"Fifty thousand dollars," I said out loud, throwing the bag over my shoulder.

This murder was starting to make a little more sense.

CHAPTER 9

My old office at the police station was almost exactly the way I'd left it a little less than three years ago. A bunch of documents had been piled on top of my desk, no doubt paperwork my colleagues had no other space for. The computer, which was already old back then, now looked like a museum piece. Or at least, what was left of it did: a scavenger had taken the monitor and keyboard, maybe the same individual who had replaced the chairs on either side of the desk with the oldest, creakiest ones in the office.

Me being there was just a formality in any case: Echeverría, Lamuedra, and I had agreed I'd keep working from my lab in the court-house. I started organizing the desk a little—just enough to let my old colleagues know I was back—when someone knocked. I turned and saw Lamuedra standing in the doorway with a woman in her thirties who I recognized as Julio Ortega's girlfriend.

"Miss Guillón, this is Officer Laura Badía. She works for both the precinct and for the court, and she'll be in charge of investigating your boyfriend's homicide case."

Noelia Guillón feebly raised a hand to greet me. She wasn't wearing makeup, and her eyes were swollen and bloodshot.

"Noelia has just come from the waterfalls in Iguazú. She took the first plane south when she was notified of the murder, to come see us,"

Lamuedra continued. "It seems Sergeant Debarnot forgot to mention that her immediate presence was not necessary."

That last bit was for me. I ignored it.

"I'm so sorry for your loss," I said. "We're going to do everything we can to find the person who did this. I am going to need to ask you a few questions when you feel better."

"We can talk now if you want."

Lamuedra and I exchanged a look.

"We don't have to do it right away, if you need time to compose yourself," I told her.

"No, now is fine."

"In that case, come this way," said Lamuedra, heading to the interrogation room.

We sat around the solid iron table, which had a metal hoop in the middle for restraining violent suspects. I picked up a small remote control and pointed it toward a camera until the red light turned on.

Before sitting down, Noelia Guillón took off her heavy winter coat. Beneath, she wore a knit red sweater and a pair of skinny jeans that revealed the figure of a woman ten years younger. On top of being an aerobics instructor who spent the whole day at the gym to get an ass as firm as a watermelon, she was clearly blessed with good genes.

I'd never admit it to anyone, but her sex appeal was one of the things that had motivated me to sleep with her boyfriend eight weeks back. Call it a competitive streak.

"Are you ready to begin?" asked Lamuedra.

"Yes," she said. With a look, Lamuedra handed the interrogation off to me.

"When was the last time you saw Julio?" I asked.

"Two nights before he was killed. We had dinner at his house. He made beer-braised chicken, my favorite dish, and the idea was to have a quiet night in. Watch a movie, all the usual stuff. It was sort of a mini going-away date, because the next day I was leaving to see the falls in Iguazú."

"Do you have any idea who could have done something like this?"

"I honestly have no idea."

"Had you noticed him behaving unusually at all?"

"Yes, definitely. He's been a little off lately."

"In what way?"

"Like, very affectionate with me. Too affectionate, almost. Like he was trying to make up for something."

"Make up for something?"

Noelia looked directly at the red camera light for a few seconds. "I think he was cheating on me with another woman."

Fuck. My heart raced. If it came out that I had been involved with Julio so recently, they would have to launch an inquiry, and I could kiss my career at the court goodbye.

I tried to calm down. I couldn't have caused that change in attitude. That was almost two months ago, and it had been a one-night thing, the product of one coincidence and about five drinks too many. After a friend's birthday celebration, we'd all gone out dancing, something I almost never did. At one point I found myself alone, and I noticed Julio Ortega standing right next to me. I felt inexplicably spontaneous, a feeling that brought me back to my teenage years, when he was the most sought-after guy in town and I was one of the many teenage girls he flirted with.

"I'm sorry to have to ask this, Miss Guillón," prefaced Lamuedra, "but do you have any suspicions as to whom your boyfriend may have been cheating on you with?"

I stood up so forcefully that my chair tipped backward onto the floor.

"What's wrong?" Lamuedra asked.

"Can we get you anything, Noelia? A glass of water?"

"No, but do you have any tissues?" she asked, wiping her nose with the back of her hand.

I nodded and started for the door, but Lamuedra raised a hand to halt me. He leaned back in his chair and pulled a pack of tissues from his pocket.

"Here you go. As I was saying, do you have any idea who this possible other woman might be?"

Noelia Guillón twisted the strap of her purse on her lap. I swallowed hard.

"I have my suspicions. That last night, when we had dinner together, I wanted to confront him about it. I told him to be honest with me, and I said that I'd forgive him, you know, that I just wanted to know the truth. But of course he denied everything."

"Who do you think it was? It's important," Lamuedra insisted.

"Julio went to the casino a lot. Always on Fridays and Saturdays, and two or three days during the week, too. One time I went with him, and I just remember that this one woman—almost an old woman—was really excited to see him. The other day someone told me that the two of them left the casino together in a taxi. But I'm sure he just dropped her off at her house and came straight home, because I was waiting for him there."

I breathed a sigh of relief. I tried not to make it too noticeable.

"He was in pretty bad shape," she continued. "He threw up twice, and he didn't open Impekable the next morning."

"Did he do that often? Stay at the casino late and then not open the store the next day?" asked Lamuedra.

"Every once in a while."

"Did he spend a lot at the casino?" I interjected.

"Sometimes. I know that some nights he lost a ton, but I never really knew how much he earned with Impekable."

"Would you say he spent too much?"

"We were just dating. We had separate bank accounts. But if I had to guess, I'd say he didn't spend more than he had."

"Let's get back to Mr. Ortega's suspected infidelity," said Lamuedra. "Do you have any other reason to suspect he was with another woman?"

"Yes. About three weeks ago, I went to his house at night to surprise him. His car was parked out front, but when I went inside, there was nobody there."

"Some people prefer to take a taxi when they go to the casino," suggested Lamuedra. "They're ashamed to have their car seen there."

"But Julio never cared about that kind of thing. And anyway, he wasn't at the casino, either, because after calling him a bunch of times, I went there to look for him. Like, I even asked some of the employees and they told me they hadn't seen him that night. So I went back to his house and parked far away, waiting for him to get back."

She interlaced her fingers and pulled until her knuckles cracked.

"He showed up at six in the morning in a hired car."

"Did he say where he'd been?"

"No. And I didn't ask. I couldn't bring myself to go talk to him."

When I heard this, all I could think was *Thank God it wasn't the night I was there.*

"Did Mr. Ortega collect arrowheads, Miss Guillón?" I asked.

Julio's girlfriend looked at me and frowned. "What?"

"Did he collect arrowheads?"

"No. What does that have to do with anything?"

"The day of the murder we found broken glass in the front hall of Julio's house. It wasn't from any broken windows or furniture. When we checked his phone, we found a photo of a display case that held a collection of arrowheads, and its dimensions matched the broken glass."

"Those arrowheads don't have anything to do with the murder," Noelia said.

"You know about the collection?"

"Yes, of course. Julio found it in a wardrobe with a fake bottom. About six months ago, he inherited a bunch of furniture from his uncle, and some of the pieces were so big and solid he decided to take them home. He found, like, a secret compartment in one of them, in the wardrobe his uncle had in his library. When Julio opened it, he found that display case."

I made a mental note to go back to Ortega's house and inspect that wardrobe.

"How are you so sure it had nothing to do with the crime?"

"Because Julio would never let someone beat him to death over some stupid arrowheads. He'd had that case leaning against the dining room wall for weeks. Some days he said he was going to donate it to the museum. It's a beautiful collection, if you know about these things. The pieces are crafted with this kind of iridescent rock that I've never seen before in any other arrowheads from this region."

"It sounds like you know more than me about lithic art," said Lamuedra.

"My parents had a really big collection. At one point they were thinking about opening a small private museum, but now they've decided to donate it to the Mario Brozoski, when it's time."

"Did you ever show your parents the arrowheads Ortega found in that wardrobe?" asked Lamuedra.

"No. I told them about the case and obviously they showed a lot of interest, and my dad said he wanted to see them, but I never remembered to bring them when I visited home."

There were a few seconds of silence.

"We're almost finished," I said. "I don't know about Commissioner Lamuedra, but I only have one more question. In the autopsy, we found circular injuries on the backs of his hands."

"Oh right, that," she said disdainfully. "He's had those for over two weeks."

"Do you know how he got them?"

"A poker bet with his friends. Once or twice a week, he goes . . . he went to play at La Preciosa."

La Preciosa was a bar that was always open and always empty, except for the not-so-clandestine poker game that had been going on in the back room for years.

"What kind of bet involves letting . . . ?" Lamuedra began, leaving the sentence unfinished.

"I asked the same question. What kind of bet involves letting someone put a cigarette out on both your hands, right? He said they got drunker than they should have and things got out of . . . er, control."

Lamuedra and I exchanged a quick look. They'd looked like cigarette burns to me, too, but Luis had been clear on that point: a cigarette couldn't have burned that deep.

Either Julio Ortega had lied to his girlfriend, or his girlfriend was lying to us.

CHAPTER 10

We found the secret compartment on our second visit to Julio Ortega's house, exactly as Noelia had described. It was empty. We also reinspected the entire house, but we didn't find anything.

Afterward, Manuel headed back to the courthouse, and I walked the two and half minutes to the house where my aunt Susana had raised me. I knocked on the green hardwood door.

"What happened to your key?" she asked.

"Hello, Aunt Susana, nice to see you, too."

"Has something happened?"

"Why does something have to happen for me to come see you?" I answered, planting a kiss on her cheek and hurrying inside to take refuge from the cold morning.

"Well, I don't know. You don't come by here very often. In fact, it was about a month ago that I bought you this. I forgot to give it to you when you came over to use up all my water."

She gestured to the corner of the dining room, where a leafy, overgrown fern was busting out of its pot.

"Aunt Susana, you really shouldn't have. You know I can't even take care of a cactus. I'm going to kill it."

"No, you are *not* going to kill it. You're a grown woman with no children, no husband, and no boyfriend. Not even a dog. You've got to start somewhere."

"You always were a tactful one."

"Maybe I'd treat you better if you came to visit me more often."

"I have so much work, Aunt Susana. I'm on the clock even as we speak."

I hung my coat on a hook by the front door, beneath a niche in the wall that held a statuette of the Virgin Mary. A souvenir from my aunt's time in the convent, just before she joined the police force.

"What are you doing here, then?"

"I came to ask for your expert advice."

"So I was right!"

I didn't know what to say. It was true, I hardly ever visited her.

"Expert advice, eh?" she repeated, grinning at me. "Don't tell me you've finally decided to learn to cook."

"I'll die first."

"Don't talk like that. God help me if I have to pay for your funeral all by myself. If only you had some other relatives I could split the cost with."

I laughed. Her two years at the convent may have turned her into a devout Catholic, but her thirty years as one of the first female cops in the Santa Cruz Province had left her with a gruff attitude and a sardonic sense of humor.

"So, you came to ask me for a favor?"

"Something like that."

"Yes, I thought so. You know it's going to cost you, right?" she said, forming an imaginary pistol with her fingers and pointing it at me.

"Aunt Susana, do we always have to have the exact same conversation? You know I can't take you shooting without a license."

"But the doctor won't *give* me one. He says with hands like mine I can't be trusted with firearms anymore. I'd like to take *him* to the shooting range, then we'd see who's really got the steadier hand."

Though she had retired eight years ago, my aunt had never gone a month without visiting the shooting range until half a year ago, when the doctor decided the arthritis had caused too much damage to her hands and declined to renew her license.

"Or we could go to the country. Put some bottles on top of rocks and shoot with the Browning," she said, referring to the 9 mm pistol carried by nearly every cop in Argentina.

"With my service weapon? You really have gone off the deep end."

"We could use mine."

"Aunt Susana! That pistol cannot leave this house. It's not even legal for you to still have it."

She raised a finger in protest but thought better of it and kept quiet.

"I came because I wanted to ask you about arrowheads," I said.

"Why didn't you say so?" she responded, suddenly jovial.

From the way her face lit up, anyone else would have thought she'd instantly forgotten about going shooting. But I knew her scheme too well. Like a child, she would behave herself for a while, then ask again.

"Do you want anything? Yerba mate?"

I agreed and she shuffled off to get her gourd. I saw a display case with several of my aunt's arrowheads on the dining room wall, and I went to take a closer look. She'd spent thousands of hours in the countryside, studying the ground, leaning forward with her hands behind her back. The stone pieces were affixed to a red velvet backing and protected under a glass pane, just like in the display case we'd found a photo of on Julio's phone. My aunt's were arranged in concentric circles, though, not in a triangle, and their coloring was much less remarkable: brown, ochre, black, and one or two milky-white ones.

I was still engrossed in the collection when my aunt came back with the yerba mate and a plate of tea cookies.

"So, you want to talk about arrowheads, eh? Just the other day I went on an arrow-hunting excursion with a group from the senior center, at an old Tehuelche campsite."

"Did you find anything good?"

"Eh. A broken arrowhead and a few scrapers. It's getting harder to find whole pieces worth hanging on the wall."

"How long did it take you to find all these?" I asked, touching the display case.

"Let's see . . . I had that case made when I was around fifty, to show off the best arrowheads I'd found at that point. I've been collecting them as long as I can remember. Before I turned fifteen, I think we went searching for them at least twice a week. I went less after my parents sent me to live with your grandmother in town so I could finish high school. But I went whenever I could, and I still do, even though I can barely bend over to pick the damn things up anymore."

I looked back at the arrowheads. I always tried to avoid making eye contact with her when she talked about her childhood. I was afraid that if she saw my face, she'd realize I knew the truth.

Her parents hadn't sent her to Puerto Deseado to finish high school. She had chosen to leave, in an attempt to get away from the hell she'd been living in for eleven years. Her stepfather had started abusing her when she was four, and continued until she was fifteen, when she put two grains of strychnine in his coffee and watched him die foaming at the mouth.

Then came guilt, God, and the convent. Two years after that, she swapped her habit for a badge and learned to thrive on the male-dominated police force. Until her niece and her niece's husband—my parents— were killed in a car accident.

Which means Susana was actually my great-aunt, my maternal grandmother's younger sister. Fifteen years younger. After the accident, she was the only family I had left. I was sixteen, so she took me in until I finished high school. She was probably also the reason I decided to enroll in the police academy.

"I wanted to ask if you could tell me about a collection that looks like this," I said, holding out my phone.

Aunt Susana did not look. Instead, she calmly refilled the yerba mate gourd from a thermos.

"So, you'll take me shooting, then?"

I sighed. The woman was insufferable when she was set on getting her way. It must be genetic.

"Fine, at some point we'll go to the countryside for target practice. But I don't know when. And don't ask me about it every time I see you."

"It's not like I see you that often anyway."

"Are you going to look at the photo or what?"

I held up the phone to show her the photo of the iridescent arrow-heads. When she saw it, she put down the gourd and grabbed my phone with both hands.

"Where is this?" she asked.

"That's what I'm trying to figure out. We found the photo on the phone of a homicide victim. I also found this in his house." I reached into my pocket and produced the iridescent arrowhead in a small plastic box, which I placed on the table. "I think it may be related to the murder."

"To lots of murders. If you believe what they say, I mean." She said it derisively, but I noticed she was keeping her hands away from the plastic box.

"Lots?"

My aunt put the phone in her lap and looked at me over her glasses. "What I mean is, if you buy into this sort of thing, it is absolutely related to all sorts of crimes. This is a photo of the iridescent arrowhead collection. People have supposedly been killing each other over it for thousands of years."

"Sorry, what are you talking about, exactly?"

She lifted her eyebrows and put a hand on my knee. "Laura, these arrowheads are supposedly very dangerous. I don't know the story very well, but there are lots of people who would tell you they have brought nothing but death and suffering since the day they were carved."

"For someone who doesn't know the story, you sure know a lot of details."

"I mean, it's really just a legend that arrowhead collectors always tell each other whenever the topic of the iridescent collection comes up."

"Uh-huh. What's the legend?"

"Well, the long and short of it is that the stone was given to the chief as a gift upon the birth of his son. When the chief saw the stone's unique colors, he gathered all his greatest artisans and ordered them to carve several arrowheads, which would be the new chief's seal when he was grown. His son's name was *Yalen*. Or *Yalen*. No one can ever agree how it's pronounced. Anyway, when he was old enough to have mastered the bow and arrow, which archaeologists calculate would have been when he was around seven years old, the chief gave him the arrows and told him that with them, he would be able to kill anyone he wanted. And he told him that when *he* had children, he was to give the arrows to the oldest at that same age."

My aunt was waving her arms around melodramatically.

"They say that when his father died and Yalen became chief, he married a beautiful woman named Aimar. But Yalen had a younger brother named Magal, who was totally consumed with jealousy. So, one day Magal stole the iridescent arrows from Yalen and used two of them to murder Yalen and Aimar in their sleep. He fled with the rest of the arrows, but he was found dead a few days later. And that was how there came to be this sort of myth that says that whoever tries to separate any of the arrows from the rest of the collection will die before the new moon."

I laughed so hard that my aunt got defensive.

"I'm not saying I *believe* it, Laura. I'm just telling you what they say. There's a collection of iridescent arrowheads laid out in a triangle shape, and whoever tries to separate them, or change their order, dies."

"You don't say. Do you know anything else about it?"

"Nope. When are we going shooting?"

CHAPTER 11

That afternoon, I went back to the morgue. The stainless steel table in the middle of the room was now empty. In a corner, Luis was removing tools from the sterilizer.

"Laura, how are you?"

"I'm good, how're you?"

Luis shook his head, walked toward me, and gently grabbed my shoulders. "No, seriously. How are you?"

"I'm fine, honestly. I don't know what to tell you about yesterday. I must have had low blood sugar or something."

"Laura, look. I know you, and I know how proud you are. What happened yesterday will never leave this room. It could happen to anyone. It even happened to me not too long ago. I earn my living doing this, but I'd gladly have taken a kick in the balls to get out of the autopsy for the Núñez kid."

I remembered the case perfectly. Joaquín Núñez was nineteen months old when his stepfather, off his ass on booze and God knows what else, suffocated him with a pillow so he'd stop crying.

"Everybody has their frayed wires," Luis continued. "Sometimes they touch. And when they do, no tough exterior or professional distance can save us. For me, it was that baby. I couldn't get it out of my head that he was just a defenseless, tiny child. I couldn't compartmentalize enough to do my job. For you, it was Ortega. Maybe he reminded you of someone. Or maybe you knew him."

I wanted to shake my head, but I couldn't.

"Whatever the reason," he continued, "this man got your frayed wires to touch."

I stared silently at the autopsy table, thinking. I felt like I understood myself a little better, like it made sense that I was thirty-two years old but hadn't had a single real relationship since high school. Or even any friends. Luis had just identified a fear that, until that moment, had been perfectly camouflaged inside of me.

Everybody has their frayed wires, I repeated mentally. Mine touched when I was supposed to take a knife to the corpse of someone who had once been part of my life. Not even a loved one or a family member— that would probably give anyone a short circuit—just someone closely associated with a happy time in my life, when I was a sixteen-year-old girl obsessing over a nice-looking guy, and my parents hadn't yet died in a horrible accident.

I took a deep breath and spoke slowly so Luis wouldn't notice the lump in my throat. For now, I had no intention of telling him or anyone else about me and Julio.

"What conclusions were you able to draw from the autopsy?" I asked.

"Well, to start with, he had a lot of alcohol in his blood. Some cocaine, too, though not much," he said, handing me the toxicology report. "Basically, he died of head trauma. There was no damage to the abdominal organs. Do you remember the marks on the back of his hands?"

"The not-cigarette burns?"

"Yeah. It turns out they weren't burns at all. I found microscopic traces of iron inside of them."

"They nailed him to something?"

Luis shook his head and gave me an uncertain expression, like he was debating whether or not to tell me.

"What was it, then?" I insisted.

"I think they were made with a drill."

"They drilled a hole through his hands?"

"I can't think of any other explanation."

We were both silent for a beat.

"Maybe they tortured him for the arrowheads," I suggested. "Echeverría's archaeologist friend says the collection is worth around fifty thousand dollars."

Luis whistled when he heard the figure.

"But the scars are from two weeks before he was killed, so the dates barely work," I said, working through it in my head. "According to the girlfriend, Ortega found the false base of the wardrobe on July twenty-first, and he died on August seventh, exactly seventeen days later. If those scars are two weeks old, that means that two or three days after he learned he had this valuable collection, they were already torturing him for it."

"That seems too soon, doesn't it?"

I nodded. If things had gone the way Julio's girlfriend said they did, it was too soon.

If they really had gone that way.

CHAPTER 12

"Her Honor wants to see you in her chambers," Isabel Moreno said as she passed me in the hallway between my lab and the courthouse kitchen. Her nails were violet, with a green flower painted on each. Only someone like her would waste time and energy on that kind of thing.

"I'm doing great, Isabel, thanks for asking," I said, opening the door to the lab to drop off my things.

I took the stairs to the second floor. The door to Echeverría's chambers was open, and laughter was coming from inside.

"Good morning," I said from the doorway.

"Here she is," Echeverría said to a man with a well-trimmed white beard who was rocking on a chair across the desk from Echeverría. "Come in, Laura, come in. This is Dr. Alberto Castro, chair of the archaeology department at the University of Buenos Aires. He's an old friend of mine and, incidentally, one of the most knowledgeable people in the world on the subject of the Tehuelche."

I greeted Castro with a kiss on the cheek. Despite the beard, he somehow still smelled like aftershave.

"Alberto lives in Buenos Aires, but for years he's been taking trips south to investigate Tehuelche archaeological sites. In fact, he regularly collaborates with the museum here in Puerto Deseado on all things lithic."

"When you put it that way, it sounds very grand," Castro said. "The way I see it, I'm a fellow who likes rocks, and whenever I can, which is usually once or twice a year, I come to work with the museum's collection."

"Alberto wasn't planning to visit until next year, but I convinced him to come early by telling him what we found in Ortega's house. Or what we *didn't* find, really."

Echeverría swiveled in her chair to address Castro.

"So, Laura—or rather, Detective Laura Badía—is our forensics expert, and she's also a Santa Cruz provincial police officer. She's in charge of investigating the Julio Ortega case."

I smiled in acknowledgment.

"Laura, I'd like you to show Alberto the arrowhead you found at the scene of the homicide. I already sent him the photo from Ortega's phone."

"Of course. Should I go get it?"

"Better if both of you go to the lab. I have to finish looking at these files before this afternoon," she said, gesturing to a pile of manila folders stacked almost as high as her open laptop.

Castro finalized lunch plans with Echeverría, went to the coatrack to recover an ungodly mass of coats, scarves, and various other forms of padding and insulation, and followed me downstairs.

I had to smile. I always marveled at how many layers Buenos Aires people wore when they deigned to venture south.

The fluorescent tubes blinked a few times before illuminating the part of the courthouse where I spent most of my time. At one end of the stainless steel table was the reconstructed pane of glass, still smudged with fingerprint powder. At the other was the fern my aunt had given me, which had somehow survived its first twenty-four hours in my custody.

"Are these the shards of glass from the missing display case?" asked Castro.

"Yeah, that much we know for sure," I said, transferring the fern to a broad shelf on the wall. "And this is the arrowhead I found about six feet away."

I unlocked my desk drawer, removed the plastic box, and handed it to Castro. His eyebrows rose as he opened it.

"This is a very special piece," he said, rotating the arrowhead between his fingers.

"Because it's iridescent?"

"Because of what its iridescence means. It's made with opal from the Amazon, a semiprecious stone from the north Brazilian rain forest. Curiously enough, it has a strength and crystallization very similar to the volcanic obsidian from this region."

"You know all that just from looking at it?"

Castro laughed and put the arrowhead down. "No, I know it because this is a famous arrowhead and I'm familiar with its history. If you showed me a photo of Marilyn Monroe and I told you she committed suicide, you wouldn't assume I knew her personally."

I remembered what my aunt had said about the iridescent collection.

"How did some famous Brazilian arrowheads end up in Patagonia?"

Castro lifted a bony finger and wagged it back and forth. "The stone is from Brazil, but the piece was made here, by the Tehuelche."

"You mean the arrowhead was carved in Patagonia with stone from the Amazon?"

"Odd, isn't it? From the technique, we can tell that this stone would have been carved between five and six thousand years ago. Needless to say, that was long before Columbus and the arrival of horses in the Americas, so the opal would have been carried more than three thousand miles by foot. From northern Brazil to southern Patagonia."

I pulled up the calculator on my phone. "At two and a half miles per hour, walking ten hours a day, that would take four months."

"Quite right. Though it may have changed hands many times through trade, in which case it would have taken far longer to reach Patagonia. Decades, perhaps even centuries. No one can say with any degree of certainty how long it took the stone to get from the Amazon into the hands of the artisan who turned it into the Panasiuk Collection."

"The what?"

"The Panasiuk Collection. That's how these arrows are known in the world of lithic Tehuelche art. Though it got that name thousands of years after they were carved."

"You're saying these arrowheads have their own special name?"

"Absolutely."

"Panasiuk," I repeated. "Sounds like the name of a chief."

Castro laughed. "You couldn't be further off. Teodor Panasiuk was a Polish immigrant to Patagonia in the 1920s. He worked in the country until he was able to buy some land near Cardiel Lake. Apparently, from the very day he arrived in Patagonia, he had a keen interest in searching for arrowheads. Then word got out that Panasiuk had found the opal arrowheads, which, with time, became one of the most famous lithic art collections in the world. Or infamous, depending on who you ask. Regardless, it's a collection that's discussed quite a bit, but of which we know very little, because until now, no one had seen it."

"What do you mean?"

"This is the first ever photo of the collection," he said, touching a printout of the image from Ortega's phone. "Or, more precisely, it's the first photo of these thirteen pieces. There are fifteen Panasiuk arrowheads in total."

"What do we know about the other two?"

"Practically everything. They were identified years ago, and they've been photographed and studied from every possible angle by me and many other scholars. One is part of a private collection, at a ranch not too far from here. The other is at the museum."

"What museum?"

Castro raised his eyebrows, surprised by my question.

"The one here, Miss Badía, in Puerto Deseado," he answered, flabbergasted. "The Mario Brozoski Museum. Though I will say, I don't think anyone there, not even the director, is aware of its true value."

He checked his wristwatch and smiled.

"Come with me. They just opened."

CHAPTER 13

The main hall of the museum was filled with arrowheads, spears, axes, and other Tehuelche stone instruments behind glass, while text on the walls behind them explained Tehuelche history and customs in technical jargon that was totally incomprehensible to the average visitor. My gaze paused on a bronze plaque that said the hall was dedicated to someone named Vicente Garrido.

"Laura, how are you doing?" asked the director of the museum, coming out from her office to greet us. It was a small town. She'd been the janitor at my high school.

"Hi, Virginia," I said. "Didn't this hall used to be dedicated to Patrick Gower?"

Patrick Gower was an Australian who provided key documents that led to the discovery of the HMS *Swift*, a wrecked British warship that lay submerged for two centuries before divers from Puerto Deseado discovered it. Before Gower visited in the seventies, nobody had ever heard of it.

I was actually pretty familiar with the story. I'd nearly had a fling with one of the divers, but he was arrested for illicit trade of cultural artifacts before it really got anywhere. I'd always had good taste in men.

"Yes, that's what it used to be called," Virginia responded after clearing her throat.

"But you changed the name?" I asked, remembering the smile on that elderly Australian's face when they brought him from the other side of the world to see the golden plaque with his name on it. Now there was a new plaque, with a new name, in exactly the same place.

"Well, you see, when Garrido donated this major collection to us, the least we could do was put his name on the hall where it's on display. So for the moment, that's Patrick Gower Hall, over there." Virginia pointed to the thirty-six-square-foot entrance hall, where the museum guestbook sat open atop a peeling Formica desk.

"Unsightly," murmured Castro between coughs. He was about a third of the way through the process of removing his many coats.

From the way Virginia glared, it seemed clear that her relationship with Castro was somewhere between bad and disastrous.

"The donation from this Garrido person must've been pretty important," I said.

"Well . . . between the arrowheads, the spears, the scrapers, and the burins, it was over eight thousand pieces. It was in the paper and on all the local radio stations. They even did a half-hour local TV special. It really is a spectacular collection, with pieces in every color imaginable. It has everything from pieces made out of broken glass bottles brought by the first Europeans to a black obsidian arrowhead this big," she said, lifting her hand and straining to stretch her index finger and thumb as far from each other as possible.

"Six months ago, the museum had a thousand-odd pieces. Imagine our surprise when Garrido's lawyer called to tell us he'd left his collection of arrowheads to *us*," she said, pointing at her chest. "Everything else, his property and money and all that stuff, went to a sister. He didn't have any children."

"Wait, he's from Puerto Deseado?" I asked.

"Of course. You must have known old man Garrido. Thin, tall. Lived in that stone house across from Antonio Oneto Elementary. He wore his hair slicked back and used to walk around with that tiny little three-legged dog."

"Ah, 'the Heron,'" I said.

"Precisely."

That man had been a town treasure. Everyone always called him the Heron. I'd never known Vicente was his first name, and I doubt anyone else had, either. But of course I knew him. Everyone knew the kindly old man who lived across from the school, in the same house where we'd found Julio Ortega's body.

"Hi, hello, you there? You okay?" asked Virginia.

"Yes, sorry, I'm good." I turned to Castro. "Are you going to show me what we came to see?"

He nodded and motioned for me to follow him. Virginia went back to her office, and we walked between the display cases filled with arrowheads and scrapers until we arrived at one that looked just like the rest: a three-foot panel containing dozens of lithic artifacts affixed to a white backing.

Castro pulled the arrowhead I'd found at Ortega's house out of his pocket and held it against the glass. With his other hand, he pointed to an arrowhead in the case. Both pieces had the same teardrop shape, and both reflected the same iridescent light.

"Do you see, Miss Badía? No one could doubt that it's from the same collection."

"You can call me Laura."

"Only if you call me Alberto."

"Deal. Was that arrowhead one of the pieces Garrido donated when he died?" I asked, pointing to the one behind the glass.

"No, the museum has had this piece for years."

"Do you know where they got it?"

He shook his head. "Things are managed very unprofessionally here," he said in a low voice, glancing at the director's office. "The people here—despite often trying their best—are municipal employees who don't receive any training at all on how to catalogue pieces and document their origins. And that's how it is today. Imagine how much worse it was twenty or thirty years ago, which is when I'd estimate this arrowhead was added to the museum's holdings."

I considered explaining Puerto Deseado's chronic budget problems and how politicians always promised municipal jobs in exchange for votes, but I figured there was nothing to gain from opening that can of worms.

"Follow me, I want to show you something else," said Castro.

CHAPTER 14

We crossed the main hall and stopped at the old printing press that had produced the first copies of the local newspaper, *El Orden*. Behind it was a door with a sign that said "Museum Staff Only."

Castro unlocked the door, and we entered a room with shelves all around the perimeter, each covered with blue plastic boxes. In the center were three tables, two of which held basins, jars, and other containers filled with objects floating in water—I assumed these were artifacts recovered from the HMS *Swift*. The third table held shards of dark rock. Above each table was a powerful lamp affixed to a moveable arm, like the kind dentists use.

"This is my worktable," said Castro, carefully moving several shards of stone to one side. He opened a briefcase he'd brought from the courthouse and removed a white folder. He flipped through the pages until he found a printout of the photo from Ortega's phone. The copy Echeverría had sent him was watermarked with the words *CONFIDENTIAL—EVIDENCE*.

"There's no question you found one of the arrowheads from the Panasiuk Collection. But even more significantly, you found this one." He placed his index finger on the photograph, right over the arrowhead in the center of the triangle. "Look at how it has the same leaf shape as all the others, but much wider."

I nodded, even though I thought they looked more like teardrops than like leaves.

"It's number five, the most famous piece in the collection," he added.

"How do you know it's number five?"

"You see, Miss Ba—Laura—the arrowheads in the Panasiuk Collection are numbered from one to fifteen," he said, flipping through a few sheets of paper until he found a diagram of the collection in which each arrowhead had a number.

"Fifteen? But there are only thirteen in the photo."

"Because they're not all in the photo. As I told you, two of the arrowheads have already been identified. We just saw one in the other room, and the other is part of a private collection, also in Patagonia. They're numbers eight and nine, respectively." He pointed at two adjacent arrowheads on the diagram.

"So, the ones in the photo are the other thirteen," I said.

"Exactly. And number five is the most famous of all, because it's considerably wider than the others. It's even thought to have been carved by a different artisan than the other fourteen," he said, lifting the arrowhead up to his eyes. "May I take a photo of it?"

"Sure, just ask me before sharing it with anyone."

Castro nodded and took two or three photos on his phone. Then he spoke almost to himself, without taking his eyes off the arrowhead: "Odd that someone would kill for the collection and leave the most interesting piece behind."

"We don't know if the murder was over the collection," I said.

"Wouldn't anything else be too much of a coincidence?"

"Possibly, but for now there's no point in that kind of conjecturing. The facts are that Julio Ortega is dead and the arrowheads are missing."

"Why do you think the glass was shattered?"

"The most plausible explanation is that the attacker was in such a hurry to take the display case that he hit it against something, which broke the glass and knocked the piece off its backing."

I said this to mollify Castro, but I wasn't actually so sure. This theory didn't square with the fact that someone had gone to the trouble of carefully sweeping up the broken glass.

Castro nodded, rotating the arrowhead between his fingers.

"How do you know that the Tehuelches carved it five thousand years ago?" I asked.

"Its age is just a guess. Arrowheads without a peduncle, like this one, were most common between the arrival of man in Patagonia, twelve thousand years ago, and the mid-Holocene period, five thousand years ago. However, the quality with which they're carved speaks to a highly developed technique that wasn't typical in the early Holocene . . ."

"Yeah, I got none of that."

Castro chuckled and apologized, raising both hands in surrender. "If they were more recent, they'd have a stem at the base. If they were older, they wouldn't be so well made."

"Why didn't you say so?"

"As for who made them," he continued, "arrowheads from the Amazon had a very different morphology and technique from the ones made in Patagonia. So the most likely theory is that they were made over here with stone from over there."

"And that's enough to make the collection worth fifty thousand dollars on the black market?"

"That and the dark history surrounding them."

"The legend of Yalen?" I asked, remembering the conversation with my aunt.

"Yes, the legend, which from an anthropological perspective is nonsense. It's an untenable story, starting with this king-like chief figure. Tehuelche leaders ruled very small groups. They didn't have a vertical social structure like the Inca, with an emperor at the head. The story is just that: a story."

"But the attacker could have acted on the story if he thought it was true."

Castro exhaled through his nose, shifted his weight on the bench, and leaned his elbows on the worktable, a few inches from the other stones, also carved thousands of years ago.

"I'm a man of science, Laura. The only thing I can tell you is that this photo matches what I know about the Panasiuk Collection: fifteen arrowheads carved in opal from the Amazon."

"In the legend, Magal took thirteen of the arrowheads, didn't he?"

"Yes, but Teodor Panasiuk had fifteen, which would include the two with which Magal supposedly killed Yalen and his bride, Aimar," responded Castro, rolling his eyes. He looked almost sickened to hear himself referring to the legend. "Those would be numbers one and two on the Fonseca Diagram."

"Fonseca?"

"He was the only archaeologist who Panasiuk allowed to study the collection. No one knows what Panasiuk saw in him. He wasn't a well-known scholar by any means. After driving dozens of archaeologists and anthropologists from his home, Panasiuk welcomed Fonseca with open arms, as if he were a long-lost relative. Fonseca sketched the arrowheads in extreme detail, capturing each of their hundreds of nicks and grooves."

Castro pointed to several sketches on the diagram.

"He also numbered them from the top to the bottom and from left to right, respecting the order that Panasiuk had given them. For each one he registered the size and weight, and even calculated the volume by submerging them in water. In his description of arrows one and two, he noted that according to Teodor Panasiuk, they were the ones Magal had used to kill Yalen and Aimar."

"How could he possibly know that?"

Castro shrugged. "I can't help you there. There are no records of Panasiuk telling anyone where he got the arrowheads. It seems that he wasn't very talkative, and they say he became even more reclusive with age."

"With all this mystery, I'm not surprised they're worth a fortune on the black market."

"Yes, and that works against us archaeologists. That's why I came to offer whatever help I can. Without getting in the way, of course. If we lose track of the collection again, it could be another half a century before it reappears. And I don't have that long to wait. This is our one chance to find it and make it available to everyone. In this museum, for example. Though I wouldn't be surprised if the powers that be wanted to take it to Buenos Aires."

"To Buenos Aires? Why?"

"Because it could answer questions that archaeologists like me have been asking our whole lives. In fact, its mere existence strengthens an article I published years ago in the *Journal of Anthropological Archaeology*, where I theorized that interactions among the people of South America were far more fluid than is commonly thought. We're talking about semiprecious stones transported over three thousand miles through tropical rain forests, mountains, the Humid Pampas, and the Patagonian Desert . . ."

That explained why Castro was so interested in collaborating: if we got our hands on the arrowheads, he would become a celebrity of sorts in his tiny archaeological world.

I thanked him for his help, though I didn't mention that, depending on the circumstances in which we found the arrowheads (if we found them at all), they would be evidence and could get tied up in a chain of custody that would make them inaccessible for months, or even years.

At least it wouldn't be half a century.

CHAPTER 15

After saying goodbye to Alberto, I went back to the courthouse. It was twenty minutes until the coffee break, when most court employees—and sometimes even Echeverría—gathered in the kitchen. I decided to answer work emails until it was time.

By the third email, I couldn't take it anymore, so I opened my browser. For years, I'd been googling everyone I met. Somehow digital voyeurism was a habit I just couldn't kick.

Google gave me four million results for *Alberto Castro*. Adding the word *archaeologist* did the trick. The first result was his profile on the University of Buenos Aires website. The background was gray, the text was Times New Roman, and Castro's headshot was at least ten years old. Just as Echeverría had said, he headed the archaeology department at UBA.

Despite the site's poor design, a quick scan of the page was enough to see that Echeverría's friend really was quite an authority. In the past few years, he had given talks in Europe, the US, and several Latin American countries. He was editor in chief of a Latin American archaeology journal and had nearly a hundred publications to his name. Most focused on the pre-Columbian peoples of Patagonia. It looked like

Echeverría wasn't exaggerating when she called him one of the world's most knowledgeable people on the subject.

I returned to the search results. Websites for archaeology and anthropology conferences, a YouTube video of a class he'd given in Mexico City, and an interview with a newspaper magazine about the cultural value of artifacts.

At the bottom of the page, I noticed a news article from 2012 in *Azul Hoy*, a local newspaper from Azul, a small city in the Buenos Aires Province. The headline didn't have anything to do with archaeology, but there it was among the other results.

YOUNG MAN KILLED IN MOTORCYCLE ACCIDENT

A young man is dead after a motorcycle accident at the intersection of Viel and Reconquista Streets late last night. Lautaro Castro of Buenos Aires, 23, reportedly lost control of his Yamaha YZF-R1 and skidded beneath the wheels of a truck carrying livestock. Castro, father to an 18-month-old daughter, died at the scene. His remains have been transported to the capital for burial. Castro was a student of archaeology at the University of Buenos Aires, where his father, Alberto Castro, is a renowned professor.

The article then inelegantly morphed into an opinion column, listing a series of similar recent events and calling on the Azul authorities to better enforce traffic regulations to prevent future accidents. There was no other mention of Alberto.

Any doubt I may have had about whether it was the same Alberto Castro vanished when I checked his Facebook page—Echeverría was our mutual friend. On his timeline was a photo of a similar-looking young man holding a baby girl. The son who had died five years ago.

I closed the browser and stepped away from my computer, feeling vaguely queasy. In all my years of social media stalking, I'd never dug up anything half that tragic.

I went to the kitchen to make a coffee.

CHAPTER 16

There was less of a mess than usual on the cheap wood table in the courthouse kitchen, and all the chairs were empty. The only person in the room was the last one I wanted to see: Isabel Moreno.

"How is everything going, Miss Investigator?" she asked with a cup of tea in her hands, leaning against the wall with an ironic smile.

"Fine," I answered, taking three steps to the coffee machine. I pressed the first button I could reach.

"Lots of work?"

"Tons."

"How's it going with the Ortega case?"

"We just started," I said, wishing the coffee maker would fill my mug already so I could get out of there.

"Well, I'm sure you'll solve it soon. Everyone's always bursting with praise for Detective Badía's brilliance. I'm sure you'll find the bad guy in a jiffy, like you did when that security guard was murdered. I mean, especially given the circumstances . . ."

Don't ask, I thought. *Do. Not. Ask.*

"What circumstances?"

The Harpy's smile peeked out from both sides of her cup.

"Well, I mean, you're fortunate enough to have some very personal information about the victim."

"Yeah, sorry, you've lost me, Isabel," I said, turning my back and pretending to look around the coffee machine for sugar.

"What I'm saying is that to investigate a crime, it must be very important to really *know* the victim, right? If you're going to catch the bad guy? Though, of course, I guess you'd have to acquire that knowledge as part of the investigation."

I strained to open the sugar packet without letting my hands shake.

"If someone were to know the victim intimately *before* the murder, that would be considered a conflict of interest, wouldn't it? If someone had a, er, *sentimental* connection with him, they couldn't maintain total objectivity during the investigation. Wouldn't you say, Miss Investigator?"

I watched the steam rising from my cappuccino and tried to assess how bad the burn would be if I threw it in her face.

"Not to mention how the victim's partner would feel when she found out the *other woman* was heading the investigation. She'd have to consider it a double betrayal, I guess. Not only to be cheated on, but then to have . . ."

I put my cappuccino on the table and took two steps toward her. In less than a second, I was right in her face. Our noses were nearly touching.

"Why don't you say your piece and be done with it?"

"Easy, Miss Investigator. Physically intimidating a colleague could cost you your job," she whimpered.

I counted to five before taking a step back. The Harpy crossed her arms and muttered something I didn't catch.

"Look, I'm going to tell you this now, and I'm going to be clear about it so there's no misunderstanding," I said, leaning on the table. "The next time you threaten me, I'm knocking out every one of your teeth. Okay? And then you can go and report me to whoever you want. But maybe, just maybe you should consider getting a life instead so you don't have to go sticking your crooked nose in everyone else's all the time."

I grabbed my coffee and started to leave. At the door, I stopped and turned around.

"And you know what else?" I added. "Quit blaming me for Campanella."

"Campanella?"

"Don't be a dipshit. It's not a good look on you. You know perfectly well that we were both sleeping with Campanella when he was here."

Campanella was an inspector from the Federal Police who had come to investigate a bag of cocaine found on a fishing boat.

"And you knew he was with both of us?"

"Yeah, from the first time I slept with him," I said, trying to rub in as much salt as possible. "You told him you didn't want anything serious. It's funny, I told him the same thing. But I was telling the truth."

"Not wanting anything serious doesn't mean you can't want to be exclusive."

"It does for me. And clearly it did for him, too."

"You're a bitch."

I nodded and took a sip of coffee, still trying not to let my hand shake. "That's good, Isabel, that's good. Better you get it all out now. That way, the next time you see me, you'll be a little more relaxed and you'll let me do my fucking job in peace."

Isabel huffed and shook her head, trying to imply that I had it all wrong. She took her tea, raised it like she was proposing a toast, and left the kitchen, giving me a shove on her way out.

"This isn't over," she said.

CHAPTER 17

The hired car agency closest to the house where Julio died was called Los Amigos. I crossed the empty parking lot and entered the small prefab building with a disproportionately large window. A Bolivian woman was sitting behind a worn desk, holding a radio transmitter. When I greeted her, rubbing my hands together to generate some shred of warmth in this midnight cold, she looked up and gave me a square-toothed smile.

"Hi, good evening," I said.

"Good evening. Did you want a car?"

"No, I came to ask a few questions, actually. My name is Laura Badía. I work for the police department."

As usual, that sentence wasn't greeted with excessive enthusiasm. The dispatcher only nodded in acknowledgment.

"How many taxis do you usually have out at night?"

"No taxis. This is a car hire service," she answered with a wry smile.

There are very few taxis in Puerto Deseado. The town is too small and the rides are too short for a taximeter to make sense. Most door-to-door transport is done by hired cars for a fixed price.

"Usually three. Four or five on weekends."

"Do you always have the same drivers?"

"Usually, yes."

"I need to speak with someone who drove nights last week, especially from late Sunday night to early Monday morning."

Noelia Guillón had said it seemed like Julio was up to something unusual. The night that she couldn't find him, three weeks before his death, he'd gone home in a hired car at six in the morning. There are only seven hired car agencies in Puerto Deseado, so I figured it wouldn't be too difficult to find the driver who had provided transportation for his nocturnal escapades, whatever they may have been.

The dispatcher brought the radio to her mouth. "Édgar and Rogelio, could you come back to the agency when you're free?"

"Will do," said one voice after a moment of static.

"On my way," said another.

While we waited for Édgar and Rogelio to get back from wherever they were—probably idling outside the casino or a whorehouse somewhere—I turned my back to the space heater to try and warm up a little. I tried to make small talk with the dispatcher but only got monosyllables in response.

The phone rang. When the dispatcher answered, she said she was sorry, but the two cars she had out that night were occupied, and she was expecting at least a half-hour wait. She gave me a look and advised the caller to try another agency.

Five minutes later, headlights illuminated the agency parking lot. The driver parked by the door and tilted his head downward. His face lit up with blue light from his phone. When I saw that he wasn't going to look back up, I started to go get him, but the dispatcher stopped me with a gesture and brought the radio back to her mouth.

"Come in for second, Rogelio."

The man turned off his headlights and came into the room, letting a gust of cold through the open door. He gave me a disconcerted look.

"I'm Laura Badía. I work for the police. I want to ask you some questions."

"I didn't do anything."

"And I didn't accuse you of anything. I came to ask for your help," I said, extending my hand.

"Rogelio Quispe," he said, shaking it.

I showed him a photo of Julio Ortega on my phone. "Do you remember driving this man recently?"

"This is the guy who got killed the other day, isn't it? Poor guy. Yeah, I used to drive him at night all the time."

"To the casino?"

"To La Preciosa, more than anywhere else."

Noelia had said Julio went there a lot.

"He played a pretty high-stakes game, I think," Quispe added.

"How do you know that?"

"He usually told me when I drove him home. If it'd been a good night, he'd say he was on fire and give me a big tip. If not, he'd say it had been a tricky night and ask to pay on credit."

The door opened and a boy with gelled hair who couldn't have been much older than twenty introduced himself as Édgar Quispe, Rogelio's son.

"Where did we always take that guy that got killed last week?" the father asked the son, looking at me, as if he wanted me to see that he hadn't been lying.

"From his house to La Preciosa or from La Preciosa to his house," the boy said.

"Did you happen to drive him early last Monday morning?" I asked.

"No, not on Monday."

Édgar repeated almost every detail of what his father had said. I asked them a few more questions, but I didn't get anything useful. I thanked them and put on my coat.

"Sometimes I took him to the casino, too," the boy said as he shook my hand.

"He liked to gamble. I already told her," the father said, glancing at me again.

"Yeah, but sometimes it wasn't to gamble. It was only, like, a couple of times, but we'd go and he'd just say to wait at the door. He'd be inside for fifteen minutes at most, and then he'd come back out. And from there always to La Preciosa. Every time. That's where he would've gone tonight, for sure."

"Why tonight?"

"It's Thursday. I almost always took him to La Preciosa on Thursdays."

CHAPTER 18

I thanked the drivers for the information and gave them my phone number, in case they remembered anything else, then ran across the parking lot to my car, which had become an icebox in the last half hour.

I had to turn the ignition a couple times before it started. Someone had told me it was the battery, or the alternator, or something like that. The problem was definitely getting worse, especially on cold nights like that one, but my glorious Corsa always came through for me in the end.

I drove the half mile to La Preciosa. Before getting out of the car, I counted eight vehicles in the parking lot, but through the window I saw only the bartender and one slow-dancing couple. Eight cars, three people.

I turned off the motor and hurried into the bar.

La Preciosa was sleazy. It smelled like cigarette smoke, and it was lit by red lights mounted on the walls. When the couple who had been dancing saw me walk in, they separated a little, even though Marco Antonio Solís's voice continued to croon through the coin-operated jukebox. The man—large, gray haired, sixtysomething—looked me up and down. The woman, thirty years younger, was wearing pants with rips up the sides. She shot me daggers with her eyes before recognizing me and raising a hand in friendly greeting. When I still worked at the station, I used to take testimony from her all the time. I hadn't seen her in three or four years, and she'd aged as if it had been ten.

I waved back, then went to the bar to order a drink. The bartender, a guy around my age with barely any hair left on his head, kept his eyes on his phone as he spoke.

"What can I get you?"

"A Heineken."

While he was getting my beer, a head peeked out from the half-open door behind the bar.

"Hey, Cucho," I said an instant after the head disappeared. He must have heard me, because from behind the door emerged the rotund figure of Cucho Soto, owner of La Preciosa.

"Laura, what are you doing here?"

"I felt like losing a few pesos at poker."

"Aw, Laura, you know perfectly well that we don't play for money here. It's a game between friends. For us, high stakes means buying the next round."

The bartender placed a green bottle on a paper napkin and slid it to me over the black Formica bar. I took a swig before speaking. The near-freezing liquid only amplified the cold I'd brought from outside, and I tried to stifle a chill.

"Look, Cucho, I didn't come here to have my leg pulled," I said. "If I want to, I can make one phone call and the five or six guys you have back there will spend the night at the station."

He opened his mouth to protest, but I continued.

"But I'm not here to make problems for you. There are lots of illegal things going on in this town, and the cops have to prioritize. I just want to talk for a few minutes. If you're willing to help me out, I'll walk out that door and drive away. No harm, no foul, no secret gambling, no hooker working at your bar."

"Get me one, too, Alfredo," Cucho said, pointing to my beer and sitting on the stool next to mine.

"This'll be easy. Just a few questions. Did Julio Ortega used to gamble here a lot?"

"Sometimes. A little more recently."

"Was he a heavy better?"

"Depends," he said, looking at his reflection in the mirror behind the bar.

When the bartender gave him his beer, Cucho grabbed a napkin from the holder, aligned it perfectly with the edge of the bar, and placed his glass directly on top, making several tiny adjustments so it was exactly in the center of the white square. Then he poured his beer and gave the bottle back to Alfredo.

"*Depends* isn't the kind of answer I need, Cucho. Was he a heavy better or wasn't he?"

"Well, okay, yes, he was. Two out of every three hands, he'd declare he had 'a good feeling about this one' and push all his chips to the center of the table."

"Did he borrow money?"

"That I don't know. I don't get involved in those sorts of things. Sometimes, Laura, it's better not to know."

"I heard he came to play about two weeks ago, had too much to drink, ended up losing a bet, and got a cigarette put out on each hand," I said, repeating what his girlfriend had told us, which I knew contradicted the autopsy results.

Cucho couldn't have looked more incredulous if I'd said Julio was abducted by aliens.

"That . . . that is ridiculous. We're grown men who have been playing together for fifteen years. We don't pull pointless stunts like that."

I nodded. "Do you know anyone who might have wanted to harm Ortega?"

Cucho took a sip of beer with his little finger pointing toward the ceiling. When he put the drink back down on the bar, he realigned it perfectly with the circle of condensation the glass had left on the napkin. That man would've taken home the gold at the Obsessive-Compulsive Olympics.

"The night that he died, a kind of strange man showed up."

"See, that's the sort of thing I'm interested in."

"Like I told you before, when we play here, it's a game between friends. Yes, we sometimes bet a little, but . . ." Cucho paused to take another sip of his beer. "What I mean is that for years, it's always been the same group of us who get together. Every once in a while, someone will bring a friend or a visiting relative, but it's not like total strangers come and join us."

"But that night someone did?"

"Yes. And he asked for Julio."

I instinctively reached into my coat pocket and took out the small notepad I carried everywhere.

"What did he say, exactly?"

"He asked if any of us knew Julio Ortega. He mainly talked to Cayota, really."

When Cucho said the name, he almost unconsciously tilted his head toward the door he'd emerged from. I saw the alarm in his eyes when he realized what I was planning to do.

"And Cayota is back there?"

"Yes, here, let me get him for you," he said, jumping off his stool.

I stopped Cucho, grabbing him by the forearm. "That's all right. I'll go to him."

I walked around the bar and pushed the door open.

A cloud of smoke and the smell of men's cologne hit me in the face. The back room of La Preciosa was cramped, with boxes of beer and wine stacked against the walls. In the middle, four men were playing poker on a green baize table with plastic chips strewn across it. To the side, on an improvised table made out of wine crates, sat thick wads of one-hundred and five-hundred peso bills.

When I walked in, one of the men snatched the money and hid it in his lap, out of my sight. The other three put their cards down on the table. All four glared at Cucho.

"Good evening. Continue, please, I don't want to interrupt. My name is Officer Laura Badía. I'm investigating the homicide of Julio Ortega."

One of the men, who had a red beard and was missing his two front teeth, squirmed a little in his chair.

Technically, I could have introduced myself as CSI Badía, Detective Badía, or Officer Badía, since I was certified to investigate crime scenes, did forensic research on behalf of the court, and was an officer of the law, but I preferred to use "Officer" when I needed to be intimidating.

"Don't worry about the cards," said Cucho, behind me. "Laura just wants to know about the guy who came asking for Julio the other day."

"Sherlock," one of them said.

"I'm sorry?" I asked.

"That's what we called him. He smoked a pipe, walked with a polished wood cane, and had a big old mustache twisted back on the ends. We figured he looked like some kind of English lord."

"He used a cane?"

"Yeah, honestly all that guy was missing was a monocle and a pocket watch," said another man, who had deep bags under his eyes and a cigarette in the corner of his mouth. No one laughed.

"That's Cayota," said Cucho.

"Yeah, delighted to meet you," I said.

I sat in the table's one empty chair. In front of me were four piles of blue chips, perfectly stacked to the same height. Clearly, this had been Cucho's spot.

The obese man who had tried to hide the money was sitting to my right, and the light hanging over the table was reflected in his wide, sweaty forehead.

"I already saw the money, you don't have to bother hiding it," I said. "I'm not interested in five men playing poker at a bar anyway. It's a free country, isn't it? I don't think you're hurting anyone. As I'm sure you'll understand, apprehending whoever beat Julio Ortega to death is the priority."

I looked at the men, one by one, and each smiled back uncomfortably.

"We need more cops like this lady," said Cayota. The man to my right nodded and put the cash back on the table. It was a lot of money.

"Cucho was telling me that on the night Julio Ortega was killed, this 'Sherlock' came asking for him."

"Yeah. Well, really, he said he heard we played poker here and asked if he could join us for a few hands," said Cayota. "Said he was passing through. Came from Calafate."

I wrote the name of the town in my notebook.

"Did he give a name?"

"He said Francisco. Pancho, for short."

"Pancho?" I asked, surprised. It wasn't the sort of nickname I'd expected for an elegant eccentric with a handlebar mustache and a cane. "What else can you tell me about him?"

"He was about sixty. Sixtysomething. Probably around five foot nine. And pretty skinny, you know, you could tell he was one of those guys who likes to stay in shape. Weird that he had the cane, since he seemed healthy and he walked fine."

"He bet like crazy," said the man with the red beard. "He wasn't any kind of poker player, but he just kept making these crazy bets all the same. From the way he looked, I guess he must've been pretty loaded. That and because whenever he lost he never cussed or anything. I didn't get it, he just smiled."

"And how exactly did he bring up Ortega?"

"We'd played . . . I don't know . . . three or four hands," Cayota hurried to answer. "Then he asked if it was always us that played together. I said yeah, it was us and two or three others sometimes. Usually Sundays, but Tuesdays and Thursdays, too."

The one who had grabbed the money felt obliged to add, "I wasn't here Sunday. I never come Sundays."

"Don't worry, Butter Biscuit, they wouldn't arrest you—you'd eat through the prison's whole food budget!" said the only one who hadn't talked, a bony kid in loose-fitting clothes with a northern accent. He was younger than the rest, and he'd been on his phone since I'd arrived.

"Are you going to tell me what he said, or are you going to keep up the comedy act?" I said severely.

The men looked at one another, disconcerted. They weren't used to having a woman talk to them like that.

"He asked like it was nothing," said Cayota. "We were just playing like normal, and he said he was buddies with a guy who was buddies with Julio. Wondered if he would come that night. I said probably, he almost always comes Sundays. Then, later, Julio keeps not showing up, and Sherlock asks what other days he comes to play. He tried to be cool about it, but we could all tell he was interested in finding him. Right, boys?"

They all nodded, except for Butter Biscuit, who repeated that he hadn't been there.

"What else can you tell me about him, besides what he looked like and that he was from Calafate?"

"He came from Calafate, but he didn't say he was from there," clarified the kid in the baggy clothes.

"Any other characteristics? His physique, the way he talked . . ."

"He was wearing lots of perfume," Cucho offered. "Carolina Herrera, I think. Besides that, we already told you everything. He looked like he was from the nineteenth century. His mannerisms, the way he dressed, the mustache."

"And you say he was in good shape physically, but he still had a cane?"

"Yeah, but I think the cane was more for show than out of necessity. Or at least, he was such a weirdo, it wouldn't surprise me."

"Okay, I'm going to see if I can get them to send a sketch artist to come from Caleta Olivia so we can try to make some drawings of what he looked like."

"You don't need to," said the bony kid, sliding his phone over the green table to me.

"Don't tell me you took his picture," said Cayota.

"I thought he looked funny. I was going to put it on Instagram, but then I decided not to."

Cayota rubbed his temples like a parent who didn't know where to begin when disciplining a child.

The photo was taken from a bad angle and the light was poor, but it still clearly showed a man with gray hair peeking out from either side of his leather beret. His mustache, also gray, was thick in the center and narrow on the ends, and the tips twisted back to point in the opposite direction. Over a plaid shirt, he wore a green vest that was a bit darker than the green of the poker table. He was holding his cards facedown, and his fingers were adorned with several gold rings. It was true: he looked like a total weirdo.

"This is great," I said to the boy, and I gave him my email address so he could send me the photo.

There was an uncomfortable silence as he sent me the image and I made sure I'd received it. I even took the time to forward it to Manuel with a brief explanation: *Possible alias: Francisco or Pancho; maybe from Calafate; expensive perfume, prob. Caroline Herrera. Possible to ID?*

"Okay, gentlemen, almost done," I said as I pressed the send button. "He never came back, I assume?"

They all shook their heads, except Butter Biscuit, who shrugged.

"How late was he here?"

"Until around three in the morning. He left in a hired car."

"Three in the morning," I repeated.

According to the autopsy report, that was just around when Julio died.

CHAPTER 19

When I left La Preciosa, I saw that the roof and windshield of my car were covered in a fine layer of frost, which glimmered under the streetlights. Fortunately, I'd been at the bar for less than an hour, so it was easy to get it off with the plastic scraper I kept under the seat for just such occasions.

After clearing the windshield, I succeeded in starting the engine after only four tries.

My two or three ideas for finding Sherlock all required talking to my colleagues, which meant waiting until the next day. I knew I wouldn't be able to sleep, so I drove the seven blocks that separated Cucho's bar from the town's biggest shithole. A legal, glimmering, garish dump. The sleaziest cesspool of them all, varnished over with fake glamour: the Puerto Deseado casino.

It was one of the few places in Puerto Deseado where you could find more than twenty people awake at two a.m. on a weeknight. The clientele varied, but one person was there every night: a man who could very well have been the reason for Ortega's lightning trips from La Preciosa.

As I walked in, I said hello to Sergeant Ulloa, the cop guarding the door that night. He was a nice-enough sub-officer who, like lots of others, needed to supplement his salary with the nighttime gigs the police force arranged, for a fee, with nightclubs, brothels, and the casino.

After briefly talking to Ulloa, I paid admission and stepped onto the casino floor. There was an overwhelming smell of women's perfume, mixed with the fainter aromas of pizza and freshly brewed coffee.

I passed hundreds of slot machines, all producing happy noises, begging me to feed them. The carpet was thick and sank beneath my feet as I walked. I took a sidelong glance at the small candy store, the few square feet of the building free of the bloodsucking machines. At the bar, atop the only occupied stool, I saw a triangular, wildly muscular man's back covered in a skintight knit sweater. That back belonged to Enrique Vera, the reason I was there that night.

The pale-faced employees in white shirts and teal vests shuffled hurriedly through the labyrinth of machines, assisting players with problems in order to minimize the time they spent doing anything other than sticking bills into the brightly lit slots.

I went up to the bar and sat a few stools away from Vera. He had short, curly hair, and he was watching a European soccer game on a screen on the wall. The glass of Fernet he was cradling in his hands looked tiny against his huge biceps.

Like every other cop in Puerto Deseado, I knew Enrique Vera. At the casino, he was almost part of the furnishings. He was always there, resting his oversized musculature on the bar. And he was always alone.

In fact, he had to be alone. His work required it. A loan shark surrounded by people tends to lose customers.

"What'll you have?" the boy behind the bar asked. He poured a cocktail and placed it on a tray, which the waitress would then take to a customer who didn't wish to be uncoupled from his machine.

"Fernet," I said, gesturing to Vera's glass and can.

The bartender put three ice cubes in a glass and poured two fingers of the dark liquor. Then he opened a can of Coke and completed my beverage. As is the custom, he gave me both the glass and the can, which was still mostly full.

"Who's playing?" I asked, looking at the TV.

Enrique Vera swiveled on his stool and gave me a dismayed look over his cantaloupe-sized shoulder.

"Atlético de Madrid and Barcelona," he answered.

When I saw him head-on, I noticed he had a skin-colored bandage on his right earlobe.

"Is it an important game?" I asked, taking my first sip of Fernet. The bitter flavor reminded me of my student days in Buenos Aires, when I was getting my degree in forensics. I hadn't had it since back then, when we called it "gasoline."

"Yeah. It was an important game. It was this afternoon, this is the replay. Any second now, Messi's going to score the first goal. Barcelona won, two–zero."

A bald man in black leather boots was descending the stairs from the upper floor. He was clearly planning on approaching Vera, but he froze when he saw me. After an instant, he regained his composure, forced a smile, and joined us.

"Doth mine eyes deceive me? Is Enrique Vera drinking . . . alcohol? And with Coca-Cola no less—full-sugar Coca-Cola!"

Both men laughed, and just then, the kid behind the bar placed a ham, mozzarella, and bell pepper pizza in front of Vera.

"Now this, this I never would have imagined," the bald man exclaimed, crossing his arms. He turned to the bartender. "You mean he's not still asking you to microwave the lean turkey breast he brings in Tupperware?"

"Sometimes you have to let yourself have the good stuff," Vera said, lifting a slice of pizza until the strings of melted mozzarella snapped. He took an enormous bite and washed it down with Fernet. "You want a slice?"

"Nah, I already ate. And look, I don't know who you are, but please give me back my friend, the real Enrique Vera, who spends the night drinking noncarbonated water and brings his food from home."

They both laughed again, and the bald man punched Vera on his gargantuan arm.

"The competitions are over until next year, Mario."

"Weren't you training for one in October?"

"It was at the end of November. But I realized I wasn't going to be ready in time."

"What are you talking about? You look like the Incredible Hulk."

"Yeah? And since when are you an expert in bodybuilding?" said Vera, chuckling and taking another swig of Fernet. "But seriously, I wasn't going to be ready for the competition in November. So now I have a month to treat myself. Pizza, ice cream, even a little Fernet every once in a while. Though I have to be careful with the drinking. My tolerance isn't up, and I get trashed after about ten seconds. Next month I'm back on the diet."

"You mean you're not going to the gym?"

"What are you, nuts? The gym's like your old lady—you love her till one of you dies."

"There he is, that's the Enrique I know! The one who'd sell his own mother to pay his gym membership."

"You know that's not what I said, fucker," he said, very softly smacking the other man on the shoulder. He did it as gently as a giant might touch a princess, afraid he might crush one of her bones.

Both men fell silent, and the bald one slyly glanced at me a couple of times. I saw him exchange a look with Vera before getting up from his stool. He'd probably come by because he needed money.

"I'll see you later," he said in a low voice before getting lost among the slot machines.

I waited for Vera to finish another slice of pizza before speaking.

"Hey, so, you come here a lot, don't you?" I asked in the sweetest voice I could manage.

"Hey, so, you work for the police, don't you?"

"But I'm off duty, and anyways . . . you have something to hide?" I almost winked, but I thought that'd be pushing it.

Enrique Vera hid his grin behind his glass, which was clouded with brown foam residue on the inside and smudged with pizza grease on the outside. He downed the rest of his drink in one gulp and returned the glass to the bar without looking me in the eyes, then did the same with the can of Coke. As if something like that would intimidate me.

"I'm going to go play a few hands," he said, getting off the stool and leaving behind more than half his pizza.

I smiled. Everyone in the casino knew Enrique Vera never gambled. He had a different role there.

"What happened to your ear?" I asked after he'd already taken a few steps. When he came back, I grabbed a slice of his pizza and took a bite.

"Night of passion. Sometimes they lose control. Not that I can blame them," he said with a smirk, slowly inserting a hand into the pocket of his very tight pants. Then he turned around and walked onto the casino floor with no apparent destination in mind, eventually getting lost behind a row of slot machines.

"There's the first goal," announced the boy behind the bar, turning his back to me so he could watch the replay of Messi scoring.

As quickly as I could, I swapped Vera's Coke can with mine. I finished my slice of pizza and took another sip of Fernet, then stood up, carrying my glass in one hand and Vera's can in the other. I walked between the machines the way you see people do sometimes, looking at each screen and trying to decide which one's about to pay out.

I left my nearly full drink on a table and, unhurried, made my way to the door. I nodded at Ulloa and stepped into the frozen night.

I was still holding the can between two fingers.

CHAPTER 20

I got to the courthouse very late the next morning, around nine. It had been almost three when I went to bed the night before, and it had taken me forever to fall asleep. I walked past the Harpy without saying hello, went into the lab, and locked the door behind me.

I put my backpack on one of the tall stools next to the stainless steel table, opened it, and took out Vera's Coke can from the night before. Then I removed the black magnetic powder from the fingerprinting kit and dusted the can, revealing several dark impressions on the red surface. I smiled: there were plenty of prints, and it would be easy to lift a few good ones.

I carefully covered each print with a piece of transparent adhesive tape, which I then removed and transferred to a piece of white card stock. In less than twenty minutes, I had twelve neat prints.

It was time to confirm or refute my theory.

My hypothesis was simple: Ortega had made his short trips to the casino to ask Vera for poker money, which he'd later been unable to repay. It wouldn't be the first time a loan shark had used physical torture to get a payment, though that sort of thing wasn't common in our town, and it had certainly never gone beyond a couple of punches or threats. There wasn't any precedent for that level of brutality in Puerto Deseado.

But my hypothesis had its weaknesses: If Vera was torturing Ortega for money, why would he have killed him? Maybe he took it further than he'd meant to? Even if that were the case, it still didn't explain the disappearance of the arrowheads. Had Ortega known how much the Panasiuk Collection was worth and offered it to Vera as payment? Would Vera have believed him?

Even if Vera's prints matched the ones we'd lifted from the broken glass in Ortega's house, we still wouldn't have all the answers. But we would be a step closer to the truth.

I also took a sample from the top of the can, where Vera had put his lips, and mailed the swab and the flakes of dried blood we'd found at Ortega's house to a friend at the Regional Forensics Laboratory in Río Gallegos. She would analyze the DNA in both samples.

Sending it straight to my friend was the only way to get results. The official method would have been impossible, since the means by which I'd obtained the saliva sample were totally illegal. The test wouldn't be admissible in court, but at least it would give me some indication of whether I was headed in the right direction.

I pulled the folder labeled "ORTEGA HOMICIDE, 8/2017" from the file cabinet and looked for the sheet with the fingerprints we'd lifted off the glass shards from the crime scene. I searched between the pages of declarations and photographs, but I couldn't find it. Then I remembered asking Manuel to take photos of the prints. He must have forgotten to put them back in the folder when he was done.

I left the lab, cursing under my breath. One of these days his carelessness was going to lose us an important piece of evidence, and I would be the one they'd throw under the bus.

I found Manuel in his office, hunched over a dismantled cell phone on his desk. He yelled at me before I had the chance to yell at him:

"What do you think this is, the FBI? Seriously, take it easy on the American movies."

"What?"

"The photo and four miserable 'leads' you sent me at one thirty in the morning. How exactly do you expect me to find this guy? That wouldn't even be enough information for the characters on *CSI* to work with. Who is he?"

"That was what I was hoping you'd help me find out. He showed up out of nowhere asking for Ortega the night of the murder. He left La Preciosa in a hired car at three in the morning."

"Right around when Ortega was killed."

"See why it's so important to find him?"

"I have no way of ID'ing him, though."

"It doesn't matter. I was just asking in case you thought of something," I said. "Where did you leave the card with the fingerprints I lifted from those shards of glass?"

"Um . . . you're going to kill me. I forgot to photograph them."

"That's not important right now. Give me the fingerprints and we'll take photos later."

Manuel raised his eyebrows, and for a second, the ever-present smile vanished from his face.

"They're in your cabinet, in the evidence folder."

"They're not there. I just checked."

"I didn't touch them," he said, flustered. "If I'd taken them, I would've photographed them."

"Maybe you took them and then got distracted by, I don't know, watching porn on your computer or something."

The smile returned to his face.

"I'm almost positive I didn't, though," he said, checking the papers on his desk and opening drawers.

"Well, keep looking, please."

I went back to the lab and rechecked the folder, the cabinet I'd taken it from, and every paper in sight. I unlocked my desk and checked every drawer. The iridescent arrowhead in its small plastic box was still there, but there was no sign of the fingerprints. I even got down on my hands and knees and looked under the furniture, but I found nothing.

After unsuccessfully searching the lab three more times, I decided to take a break. Maybe it would help me think clearer. And anyway, my stomach was growling because I'd skipped breakfast, and I thought that some coffee with lots of sugar might do me good.

Two wonderful things happened when I entered the kitchen. First, Isabel Moreno wasn't there, which was always enough to put me in a good mood. Second, someone had left a large box of cookies on the table.

I gobbled down a couple of cookies dipped in coffee and spent a few minutes chatting with an administrative assistant who had come to heat up water for yerba mate. I made myself another coffee and went back to the lab.

I was checking the cabinet for the fourth time when I heard two knocks on the door. I opened it to find Manuel leaning against the frame, holding out his empty hands.

"You didn't find it," I said. "Shit."

"You'll find it, calm down. Sometimes it helps to change your perspective a little," he said, and took Julio's phone out of his pocket.

"You found something else?"

"I got into his email."

I sat up in my chair. From the pride in his voice, I could tell he'd found something juicy.

"Only one of the messages I've been able to decrypt so far mentions the arrowheads. But it's a very good one."

He put the phone on the stainless steel table and slid it to me like a cocktail. I caught it and read the email on the screen:

TO: cornalitodelsur@yahoo.com.ar
DATE: Friday, August 04, 2017, 11:37 AM
SUBJECT: Since I know you like arrowheads

Hi Ariel,

How have you been? We haven't talked in years, so I'm not sure you'll even remember me, but I wanted to write because I moved six months ago, and last week I found a collection of arrowheads that looks pretty unusual in the bottom of a wardrobe. I'm attaching a photo.

Since I know you buy and sell antiques, I wanted to ask how much you think it might be worth. I don't know shit about arrowheads, but I've never seen any that were iridescent like these. It's like they're made out of some kind of special rock.

Anyway, I don't know if you even still live in Caleta Olivia, but if you're in the area, why don't you come spend a weekend in Puerto Deseado? Even if the arrowheads end up being plastic, it'll be a good excuse to reconnect and go get some good steak. My treat.

All the best,
Julio

"Do you see the date?" Manuel asked after I'd finished reading.

"Yeah, August fourth, two days before he was killed. There was no reply?"

"There was. That same day, at 1:53 p.m., a little over two hours after Ortega wrote to him."

"What does it say?"

"I don't know. I haven't been able to decrypt it yet. The computer is still working, but it might take a while."

"How long?"

"No idea. It could be today, or tomorrow, or sometime this year, depending on how much success we have with the brute-force algorithm."

I huffed and crossed my arms.

"So, two days before he was killed, Julio didn't know how valuable the arrowheads were," I said.

"That means it wouldn't make sense to beat him to death over the collection, right?" Manuel said, frowning. "If someone showed up at my house and threatened to beat the shit out of me if I didn't let him have my rusty frying pan, I know I'd give it to him. Why let him fuck up my face over something worthless?"

"Out of pride, maybe. It's your rusty frying pan, after all."

"Yeah, but pride has a way of becoming less important once your face looks like the Cueva de las Manos."

"Lots could have happened in those two days. We need the decrypted reply to this email as soon as possible. See if you can at least find out who cornalitodelsur@yahoo.com.ar is."

"Laura, you're running off to buy a pack of gum, but I'm already blowing bubbles," he said, handing me a sheet. "I found his real name on an antiques forum."

"Ariel Ortiz?" I asked, recognizing the black-and-white photo.

"You know him?"

It had to be some kind of cosmic joke. In addition to sleeping with the murder victim, I'd also flirted with the recipient of that email.

"Unfortunately, yes," I said.

◆ ◆ ◆

I spent the rest of that Friday arranging my meeting with Ortiz. After dozens of phone calls and a few emails, I managed to set up an interview for Sunday, though it wasn't easy. It isn't usually easy to meet with a man over a hundred miles away. It's even harder when he's an inmate at one of the most remote prisons in the country.

CHAPTER 21

At seven in the morning, the dining room at the Isla Pingüino Hotel smelled like coffee. Five or six guests sat at polished wooden tables, eating breakfast. Almost all of them were men in their fifties, who I guessed must have been managers at one of Puerto Deseado's fishing companies or at the Cerro Moro gold mine. It was Saturday.

Behind the bar, a boy in an embroidered vest and white shirt wrestled with the espresso machine. A few feet away, a man in a shirt and tie was leaning against the bar, watching the dining room.

"Good morning. Here for breakfast?" he said when I approached the bar.

"No, thank you. My name is Laura Badía, I work for the police and for the Court of First Instance. Are you Adrián Gálvez?"

"Yes," he answered, a little confused.

Questions like that sound odd in Puerto Deseado. Everyone knew he was Adrián Gálvez, the owner of the Isla Pingüino Hotel. Everyone knew who all the big businessmen in town were. He probably knew who I was, too—he couldn't have been more than five years older than me. I'd probably danced with him at the Jackaroe ten or fifteen years back.

"Is something the matter?"

"I'm investigating the murder of Julio Ortega."

"Oh, it was terrible what they did to him," he said, sipping his coffee.

"Do you remember this man staying at your hotel last weekend?"

On my phone, I showed him the photo they had given me at La Preciosa. If Sherlock really was as elegant as he tried to look, there were only two hotels in town where he might have stayed. One was Los Barrancos, where Alberto Castro was staying. The other, closer to the scene of the murder, was Isla Pingüino.

The hotel owner stared at the photo for several seconds, then slowly nodded. "Yes, he stayed here for one night."

"Last Sunday?"

"I believe so. We can check," he said, coming around to my side of the bar. "But I don't think this guy had anything to do with the murder. He was an older man, and he seemed very proper. Wasn't Ortega beaten to death?"

"I'd like to speak to the receptionist who was working that night."

"That would be Diego," he said, pointing with his chin to the youngish man behind the reception desk, outside the bar. "Normally he only works nights, but the boy who usually takes the morning shift is out sick, so Diego's working till noon. I guess it's your lucky day."

I couldn't say the same for Diego: the bags under his eyes and his wrinkled clothes made it very clear that his shift should have ended a few hours ago. He had a large head and teeth like a mouse. I went over to introduce myself and asked what he could tell me about Sherlock.

"He was only here one night. He checked in around eight and didn't come back to the hotel until almost dawn," he said, taking a sip of black coffee.

"What time?"

"I guess around three or four in the morning."

"How did he look when he got back?"

"Like he'd had a few drinks. He wasn't drunk, but he was slurring his speech a little and a couple of his shirt buttons were undone."

"Any bloodstains?"

Both the receptionist and the hotel owner were clearly startled by my question.

"No, not that I remember, no. But we could check the security footage."

"Don't you need some kind of court order for that?" Gálvez interjected, giving me an icy look.

"Only if you don't want to show me on your own."

"No, it's not that. There's just the question of my guests' privacy. If someone comes and asks for a room, we give them a room. We don't ask for their marital status or anything like that. I'm not sure if I'm being clear."

"Perfectly. But don't worry, even if the footage is good enough to extort half the town, that's not something the police here are interested in yet."

"There's also . . ."

"It also wouldn't be the first hotel in the world where people take prostitutes, if that's what you're worried about."

"No, no," said Gálvez, showing me his palms. "Not at all."

I smiled but stayed silent until things got uncomfortable—a trick that nearly always worked for me. After a few seconds, Gálvez sighed, lowered his hands, and nodded at Diego, who pulled up the footage on his computer. I walked around to look over his shoulder.

There were four black-and-white images on the screen. The first was the hotel lobby, with the camera pointing at whoever walked through the door. The second was the parking lot, and the other two were identical hallways with doors on either side.

"Sunday night. Or really, Monday morning."

Diego moved the cursor to three a.m. and started fast-forwarding through the footage. If it weren't for Diego's head, which bobbed slightly, and the occasional headlights shining through the glass door, I would have thought I was looking at still photographs.

When the time stamp in the corner was approaching three thirty, the mustachioed man appeared in the frame for a fraction of a second.

"There he is," all three of us said at once.

Diego rewound to that instant: 3:27:42 a.m.

It was absolutely the man whose photo I'd gotten at La Preciosa. He rubbed his hands together as he walked into the lobby, then said something, smiling under his mustache.

"These videos don't have sound, but I'm sure he's making some comment to me about the cold."

Diego's hand appeared, handing a key to the man, who thanked him with a slight nod before walking out of the frame. Ten seconds later, he reappeared in one of the hallways.

The way he walked with the cane was odd. He didn't use it to support his weight at all. He was well built, with wide shoulders. He looked like he'd been pretty fit when he was young.

When we played the footage again, I counted twenty-one steps. The cane didn't even touch the floor for eight of them.

"That's room 104," said Diego, pointing to the door the man had unlocked.

"I don't suppose you have cameras in the rooms?"

Gálvez gave me a scandalized look.

"And he didn't go back out that night?"

"No," said Diego.

"Do you think you might have gotten distracted for a second? Or fallen asleep?"

"I don't think so, but the easiest way to know for sure is to keep watching the video."

He pressed the fast-forward button, and the footage returned to its former breakneck speed. We watched six hours in fifteen minutes. Then Sherlock reemerged from his room for breakfast.

"Does that room have a window?"

"Yes, a little balcony that faces the street," said Gálvez, pointing to the fence on the other side of the hotel's glass door. "People usually use it to smoke."

I thought for a minute, watching the images from the security camera. Now they just showed a mob of people eating breakfast in fast-forward.

"What information do you get from your guests?"

"Name, address, and a copy of their national ID."

Without me asking, Diego started rifling through a folder so full it was about to burst.

"Francisco Menéndez-Azcuénaga," he said. "From Calafate."

Francisco from Calafate. Just like they'd said at La Preciosa.

"Make a copy of that for her, Diego. And of his ID, too."

"We didn't make a copy of his ID."

"What do you mean, we didn't make a copy?" bellowed Gálvez.

"We have his info and his signature and a copy of his driver's license, but not his ID."

Gálvez spoke to me in an apologetic tone: "Sometimes, when people come from far away and forget their ID, we give them a room if they can show us something that more or less verifies their identity."

"It's not a problem," I said. "Did he pay in cash?"

"Yeah, and he left a big tip, too, because I canceled his other nights without charging," said Diego.

"What other nights?"

"The other two," he said, showing me a spreadsheet on the screen. "He reserved three nights but then said that something had come up and he had to leave. He said to charge him for the other two nights if we had to, but Adrián told me not to."

"He was clearly a well-heeled type," said Gálvez. "We like to keep those kinds of customers happy."

CHAPTER 22

At the courthouse, I leaned back in my chair and put my feet up on the desk. I was looking at the photocopies they had given me at the hotel: Francisco Menéndez-Azcuénaga's reservation for three nights, his receipt for one, and his driver's license.

I looked at the ceiling and sighed. Small-town driver's licenses were easy to forge in Argentina. The government had been talking about creating a unified national license for years, but it was 2017 and licenses were still made of thick paper, printed on a typewriter, with a glued-on photo. And every town had its own design.

I sank back in my seat. If the license was real, he was born in 1945 and lived in Calafate. I noticed the card specified the bearer's blood type, to help first responders in case of a car accident. Menéndez-Azcuénaga was A-negative, the same as the drop of dried blood we'd found at Ortega's house.

I turned on my computer and googled his name. The results made my jaw drop. The very first link was an article from the Río Gallegos newspaper *Latitud 51*, with the headline "Important Lithic Art Collection Open to Public in October." It included a photo of the man who had asked about Ortega at La Preciosa. According to the article, Francisco Menéndez-Azcuénaga, a native of Calafate and collector of stone Tehuelche artifacts, had decided to open his home to the public so that the community could enjoy his private collection. It was one of the largest in Patagonia, consisting of over twelve thousand arrowheads and other pieces that his family had collected from the middle region of the Santa Cruz Province over the course of three generations.

The middle region of the province, I read again. According to Castro, Panasiuk had found the iridescent arrowheads in the Cardiel Lake region, smack in the middle of Santa Cruz.

My phone rang, interrupting my thoughts. The screen showed a photo of Luis Guerra with his wife and daughter.

"Luis, how's it going?"

"Hi, Laura. Hey, listen, I just had a meeting with my other boss."

"The director of the hospital? Don't tell me he finally convinced you to go full-time at their morgue."

"Never. I'll be working in both of this town's morgues until the day I die."

"That's the day you'll finally end up in one or the other, though."

Luis chuckled, then cleared this throat. "Laura, do you remember the injuries on Ortega's hands? The ones that looked like burns but had actually been made with a drill?"

"Of course."

"Well, when I was wrapping up my meeting with the hospital director, I asked if he'd seen any patients with that kind of injury recently."

"And?"

"And, a few months back, a middle-aged man checked himself into the ER with drill wounds on both hands. He said it was an accident and didn't want to report it to the police, but none of the doctors believed him. You can't accidentally give yourself a wound like that in both hands."

"What was his name?"

"The director wouldn't tell me. He said he was a middle-aged man who worked for the government."

"Luis, between teachers, cops, and administrators, half the town works for the government."

"The only other details he would give me were that he had a possible gambling addiction and a stomach ulcer caused by severe stress."

"It wouldn't be the first time a gambler who can't repay his loan shark ends up in the ER."

"It might be irrelevant, but I thought you'd like to know."

I thanked him and kept the phone up to my ear, even after he'd hung up. The conversation only bolstered my theory that Ortega had been killed over a gambling debt.

Fortunately, the results from the (totally illegal) DNA test I'd had my friend in Río Gallegos do would be arriving soon.

CHAPTER 23

The town was silent early the next day, like it is every Sunday morning. I pulled open the curtain and saw the street was covered in white frost that hadn't yet been disturbed by a single boot or tire. It was just beginning to melt under the sun's first feeble rays.

I had a hell of a time getting my car to start. I turned the ignition. *Click.* Again. *Click.* I tried dozens of times until the Corsa's hood finally began shaking, then stabilized into a regular purr. Everyone said it was "just a matter of time," and I was starting to believe them. I promised myself that I'd take it to a mechanic when I got back from the trip.

The straight, deserted drive took two hours and fifteen minutes, which I spent listening to Soda Stereo. I could tell I was approaching Pico Truncado when the silhouette of train cars leaving the cement factory appeared on the horizon, and when I started noticing plastic bags snagged on the wire fence along the road.

In town, I drove straight to the prison security booth, which peeked over the low houses. I parked in front of a gray wall topped with barbed wire and walked up to the black metal gate.

"Name?" crackled a voice through the intercom before I had a chance to press the button.

"Laura Badía. I'm from the court in Puerto Deseado."

"One moment."

I was expecting the gate to buzz and open, but it didn't. A minute passed, then I heard the metal click of the lock. On the other side, I was greeted by a police officer who couldn't have been older than twenty.

In the middle of the gray-dirt prison yard, a fraying Argentinian flag flew on top of a towering pole. Behind it was a brown building with very small windows.

The officer escorted me inside. I filled out some paperwork and went through airport-like security.

"Oh, what, you're not going to pat her down like you do me?" shouted a woman, pointing at me. She stood beside the metal detector as a female officer felt her legs, arms, and torso. "What, she's some kind of princess or something?"

"This way," said the sub-officer who had opened the gate.

We stepped into a cream-colored hallway, stopping in front of a window. On the other side, in a large, well-lit room, there were a number of chairs and nothing else. Some were arranged in groups of two or three, and others in circles of more than ten. More than half were empty. Of those that remained, inmates sat in a few, and the rest were occupied by family members who had made the trek of at least a hundred miles for Sunday-morning visitation hours.

"Visits are usually in this room," said the cop, gesturing for me to follow him down the hall, "but since you're from the court and Ortiz has a record of good behavior, we're letting you see him in his cell."

At the end of the hall was an iron door painted white. The officer placed a key in both of the door's locks and opened it with a shove. Fifteen feet later, he repeated the operation on an identical door.

"Look ahead as you walk," he suggested.

We entered a large, extremely bright cellblock. From both sides came a slew of whistles and catcalls, which ranged from the commonplace *mamita* to proposals of necrophilia.

"This isn't my first time in a prison," I told my guide in a low voice. "If these boys want to scare me, they're going to have to try a little harder."

"Cell thirty-seven," he announced, ignoring my comment.

Ariel Ortiz gave me a tired smile without getting out of bed. "So, it's true, you came."

I nodded. The cop opened the cell, let me through, then closed the swinging iron-bar door behind me.

"Tell me when you're ready to leave. I'll be waiting here," he said.

The cell was about ten feet by seven feet. Beside the bed, against one of the sidewalls, was a sink, and next to that was a curtain that I assumed concealed the toilet. Apart from that, there was barely enough room for the table and single wood chair.

I sat down and glanced at the book on the table: *Impeccable: The Most Incredible Diamond Heist in History.*

"I have to say, Ariel, even when they don't let you do your thing, you waste no time in studying up on how other people do it," I said.

"Oh, that book's just to pass the time," he said. "Diamonds have never been for me."

It was true: gemstones had never been Ariel Ortiz's particular corner of the black market. He had, however, managed to become Argentina's most infamous trafficker of antiques and artifacts. As a teenager, he had helped discover the HMS *Swift*, and he and his fellow divers had agreed to create a museum with their findings. But almost as soon as they found the ship, Ariel began taking secret solo dives to recover pieces that he would later sell to antiques dealers in Buenos Aires. Nobody would have found out if it weren't for an unfortunate coincidence, which the town was quick to chalk up to divine intervention: on one of his trips to the capital, he tried to sell an hourglass from the *Swift* to a dealer who had family in Puerto Deseado.

At the time, the entire Santa Cruz Province wanted to take him to court for plundering an archaeological site, but it never came to anything. That impunity may have been what led him to choose his particular career. Everyone in Puerto Deseado knew that Ariel Ortiz bought and sold "old stuff."

In any case, the dexterity with which he ducked run-ins with the law was impressive until a little less than three years ago. He was trying to send a container to the Netherlands from Puerto Deseado when his cargo was inspected by the cultural heritage division of the Federal Police. Between bales of extremely low-quality wool, they found nearly two tons of petrified logs and pinecones, along with nearly half a ton of Tehuelche arrowheads, spears, and other artifacts.

We had just become friends when he was arrested. Friends with a clear view to becoming something more, but friends all the same. It was a few months after I'd moved from the police force to the court, and I was happy with my job and my life. Then Ariel showed up with his big, seductive lips, his refined manners, and his stories of scuba diving and sunken ships.

"I brought you some stuff," I said, tossing a plastic bag on the bed.

Ariel opened it, trying not to look too interested, and pulled out a pack of cigarettes. He put one in his mouth and lit it with a lighter from the room's only shelf.

"Thanks," he said, exhaling smoke.

"How are you?"

"Well . . . what can I say. The food is good. The showers, not so good."

He spoke with a smile, his eyes fixed on the cigarette. He held it between his thumb and index finger, with the burning end pointing toward him, almost touching the palm of his hand.

"You must have some reason for coming to see me after two and a half years, surely?"

"Someone sounds bitter."

"Does that surprise you?"

"Ariel, we went out to dinner twice. That's it. Nothing ever happened."

"But it would have."

"Maybe, but it would have been cut short as soon as I found out about all the hustles you were running. Did you forget that I'm a cop and I work for the court? Getting involved with you would have been professional suicide. Not to mention staying in touch after you were arrested."

It was half-true. I had been charmed by Ariel, and if he had been a free man two or three weeks longer, something probably would have happened. But shit went down the way it went down, and there was no point wasting time on alternate realities.

And anyway, I got over Ariel quick, mainly because a few months later that federal agent showed up to work on the cocaine case. With him I actually got somewhere, though that story also ended badly. Not just because of where he and I left things, but because he left me with a pain in the ass named Isabel Moreno. In conclusion, 2015 was a year of extremes for me, and when it came down to it, I had it pretty rotten with the good guy as well as the bad boy.

Ariel curled his lips around the cigarette and blew smoke a few inches from the burning end, making it glow brighter.

"It was three times," he said.

"What?"

"We went out to dinner three times."

We were silent for a beat.

"Whatever, that's all over," I finally said. "I came here to ask for your help."

"Unless you're trying to buy a phone card, I don't see how I can help you."

"I came to ask you about the Panasiuk Collection."

Ariel erupted into smoky laughter. "Is that so. Do you want me to help you find Atlantis, too?"

"I don't see what Atlantis has to do with it. I came to see you because you're the most renowned arrowhead trafficker within five hundred miles of here."

"You flatter me," he said, tipping an imaginary hat, "but even if everything they say about me were true, I deal in real arrowheads. The kind made out of stone, the kind you can touch. The Panasiuk Collection doesn't exist. It's a story someone made up that took on a life of its own. Like Atlantis."

I lifted my thighs a little off the chair to pull a piece of paper from my back pocket and tossed it onto Ariel's lap. He stared at it in silence for half a minute.

"This . . . where did you get this?"

"Looks like you're still asking all the wrong questions. Is it the Panasiuk Collection or isn't it?"

"It looks like it. The arrangement and composition of the arrowheads match the sketches I've seen."

"How much would they be worth on the black market?"

Ortiz looked back at the photo. "This collection isn't complete. It's missing two arrowheads. The eighth and ninth."

I didn't tell him I already knew that from my conversations with Alberto Castro.

"So, how much?"

"Well, even incomplete, I personally know people in Europe who would pay three hundred thousand euros."

That was much higher than Castro's estimate. I was sure Ariel's was more accurate, given his background.

"And for the whole collection?" I asked.

Ariel looked at me over the sheet of paper. "If I had to hazard a guess, I'd say over a million euros for all fifteen. Maybe two million. It's hard to put a price on something that's never been sold and may not even exist."

"More than a million euros," I repeated.

Ariel nodded as he reached for the lighter again.

"And you told Julio Ortega all this the day they killed him?"

Ariel's eyes widened.

"I'm talking about the email he sent you two days before he died."

"What email? They only let us use the computer here once a week. I get Wednesdays. Ask them when you leave. I didn't respond to that email because by the time I read it, every newspaper in Santa Cruz was reporting on his death."

"Bullshit. You wrote back exactly ha and sixteen minutes after he emailed you."

Ariel's mouth fell open, making it even bigger. "I didn't have anything to do with what happened to Julio. How could I? Look where I am."

"I know you wrote back, but we haven't been able to decrypt the message yet. It's just a matter of time, though."

"I told him the arrowheads might be worth something. I told him to let me find a buyer."

"They could be worth 'something'? You were just talking about hundreds of thousands of euros."

I felt stupid before I even finished the sentence. Obviously, Ariel was going to get a buddy to buy the arrowheads off Julio for a song, then resell them at their real market value.

"Who'd you get to buy them?" I asked.

"A friend. An old client, really."

"What's his name?"

"You know I can't step on another fireman's hose."

I leaned toward the bed, reaching for the handle of the plastic bag, which held four cartons of cigarettes. Before I could pull them away, Ariel's calloused hand landed on my forearm. When I looked up, his eyes were fixed on mine, our faces only a few inches apart.

"Menéndez-Azcuénaga," he said. "His name is Francisco Menéndez-Azcuénaga. He lives in Calafate."

CHAPTER 24

Commissioner Lamuedra got up from his chair across from the judge's paper-strewn desk. He paced back and forth with his arms crossed, eventually leaning his hips against the courthouse safe, directly beneath the painting of personified numbers getting rowdy at a bar.

"Let me get this straight," he said. "Julio Ortega contacts an imprisoned antiques trafficker, who puts him in touch with this Menéndez-Azcuénaga guy, who travels to Puerto Deseado from Calafate two days later and asks about Ortega at an illegal poker game. That same night, Ortega is found dead."

"It wasn't just the same night," noted Echeverría, without turning from the window of her chambers where she was looking out at the estuary. "Menéndez-Azcuénaga left La Preciosa at the exact hour that the autopsy says Ortega was murdered."

"But the security footage from the hotel shows that he went to his room at three thirty in the morning and didn't leave until breakfast," I said. "And I sent an officer to interview the driver who took Menéndez-Azcuénaga from La Preciosa to the hotel. They didn't make any stops."

"Could the driver be lying?"

"No," I answered. "He gave us his phone, and Manuel downloaded his GPS data. They took exactly the route the driver described."

"But even if the driver isn't lying, how do you explain the blood?" Echeverría charged. "Ortega was O-positive and so was the blood surrounding the body. But near the door you found that drop of A-negative blood, which is the blood type on Menéndez-Azcuénaga's driver's license."

"That could just be a coincidence," I argued. "Six percent of Argentinians are A-negative."

"Six percent isn't so high," said Lamuedra.

"Okay, let's say he did it," I said. "That would mean he somehow snuck out of his hotel room without being seen by the cameras."

"The only way to do that would be from the third-floor balcony," said Lamuedra, "but he's over seventy and walks with a cane."

"A cane he hardly uses," argued Echeverría.

"It's true," I ceded, "but lots of elderly people walk with a cane because it makes them feel safer, even if they can walk fine without it. But it doesn't really matter—I doubt someone his age could do what they did to Ortega, no matter what kind of shape he's in."

"But wouldn't anything else be too much of a coincidence?" said Lamuedra. "This guy shows up out of nowhere and asks for Ortega at exactly the date and time that Ortega dies. There has to be a connection."

"Could be," I said. I was keeping the events relating to Enrique Vera to myself. Bringing him up would mean admitting a whole slew of irregularities to both of my superiors: I'd illegally gotten his fingerprints and a saliva sample, I'd ordered an unauthorized DNA test, and I hadn't been able to compare the prints from the display case because I couldn't find them anywhere in the courthouse. Any one of these infractions would have meant a reprimand and several days' suspension. Together, they would have spelled the end of my career in Puerto Deseado.

"You need to go talk to this Menéndez-Azcuénaga," settled Lamuedra, grinning. "You'll have to suck it up and spend a few days in the mountains."

He knew that the mountains were my place in the world. I spent about 90 percent of my vacation days there, and a few years back, when

I was doing police work, I'd asked him what paperwork I needed to fill out to get a transfer to a more remote town.

"Obviously I'd love to go to Calafate," I said, "but what are we going to tell him? That he's a suspect even though we don't have any proof? All it'll do is put him on alert."

"What do you think, Echeverría?" Lamuedra asked the judge, whose attention was now fixed on her computer.

"I don't think we'll need to come up with any explanation. He just invited us to his house."

"What?"

"*Your Honor,*" Echeverría read out loud, "*I am writing to inform you that I possess information pertaining to the disappearance of the iridescent lithic art collection commonly referred to as the 'Panasiuk Collection.' I believe this information may shed some light on the case of the murder of Julio Ortega in the town of Puerto Deseado. Regrettably, my physical condition prevents me from traveling, so I invite you (or whomever you may choose to send on your behalf) to my residence in Calafate so that I may tell you what I know. Please find my address below; I will be glad to receive you at any time. It would be difficult to share this information over the phone or via email, and so I implore you to send someone in person. Sincerely, Francisco Menéndez-Azcuénaga.*"

"He just happened to send this as soon as we start talking about him?" asked Lamuedra.

"No, this is from three days ago. He sent it to the general court email address on Friday afternoon. Isabel must have already gone home by then, because she only just forwarded it to me this morning."

CHAPTER 25

At six forty-five the next morning, two hours after picking Alberto Castro up from Los Barrancos Hotel and leaving Puerto Deseado, the patches of snow on either side of the country road reflected the first glimmers of sunlight through the windshield. There was no ice on the road, but I still tried to stay alert, keeping both hands on the wheel and not going over seventy-five. I also didn't feel totally comfortable driving a Ford Focus. I would have rather taken my Corsa, but I was afraid that its periodic inability to start would have left us stranded halfway to Calafate, so Lamuedra had assigned us a police vehicle for the trip.

"Twelve hours? I thought it was less than that."

I smiled at Castro's question. He was leaning forward in the passenger seat, rummaging through the various yerba mate accoutrements he was holding between his feet.

"You have to take kind of a Z-shape route to get there, so it ends up being around six hundred miles. If they paved the route from Puerto Deseado to San Julián and the one that bisects Santa Cruz at Piedrabuena, it'd be one hundred miles shorter."

The day before, after receiving the email from Menéndez-Azcuénaga, we had decided that I would be the one to visit this arrowhead collector. That afternoon, Echeverría had asked if Castro could tag along.

"He might end up being quite helpful. And on the way, you two can visit the Perito Moreno Glacier, which he's never seen," Echeverría had said.

I wasn't really sure whether Castro's interest was archaeological or touristic, but in any case, the two of us were driving a police vehicle to the opposite corner of the province to talk to Menéndez-Azcuénaga, and "on the way" we would see one of the world's most famous glaciers.

Around noon we stopped in Piedrabuena to have lunch and stretch our legs. We had been driving for over five hours and weren't even halfway there. My phone rang just when they brought the check. It was Echeverría.

"Hi, Laura, how's it going?"

"Good. We're in Piedrabuena. Just finished eating."

"Question: Where are the fingerprints you lifted from the broken glass in Ortega's house?"

"They should be in the cabinet in my lab. There's a folder with photos and other documents from the scene," I lied. The prints had been lost for four days, and Manuel and I had no idea where to look.

"Manuel just looked and said they're not there."

"Ah, then I must have left them in one of my desk drawers."

"They're locked. Where's the key?"

"In my pocket."

"You don't have a copy somewhere?"

"No," I lied again. There was a duplicate taped under my computer keyboard.

"Laura, are you seriously telling me that you leave town without giving us any way to access evidence for a case that we're working on around the clock? Now I'm going to have to either call a locksmith or force the drawers myself with a crowbar. There isn't room in the budget for breaking courthouse furniture."

"I'm sorry, Your Honor." I only called her that in extremely formal circumstances. "We'll be back the day after tomorrow . . . can it wait until then? What do you need the prints for?"

Echeverría sighed. "To compare them with the prints of some hoodlums a neighbor saw near Ortega's house on the night of the murder. It's just a gang of preteens, really, almost all of whom we've seen before for shoplifting, mugging, that sort of thing. I doubt it's related, but I'd like confirmation."

"So . . . can it wait until the day after tomorrow?"

"And what do you propose I do with these four children? Keep them locked up at the station? Or set them loose on the town?"

I said nothing. It seemed like Echeverría was voicing these questions more for herself than for me.

"Okay," she said, as if I'd offered a solution. "But this is the last time you leave town without giving us a way to access evidence."

"Of course, Your Honor. It won't happen again."

She hung up without saying goodbye, and I sighed with relief. Or maybe exasperation. Where the fuck were those fingerprints? What kind of excuse could I come up with in the two days before we got back to Puerto Deseado?

"Problems with Delia?" asked Castro, who had been looking at his phone during my conversation with Echeverría.

"No. Nothing serious."

I paid the bill with my personal credit card. If I was lucky, it wouldn't be more than two months before the court reimbursed my travel expenses.

◆ ◆ ◆

Within half an hour, we had left the fertile green Santa Cruz River valley and entered the flat gray mesa.

"It's a hell of a haul to talk to a guy who was in Puerto Deseado only a few days ago," I said. "He literally lives on the other side of the province."

"But he's quite an important collector. I've heard his name before. And anyway, considering where he was when they killed Ortega, I'm sure he'll be useful to you."

"Oh, I'm sure. It's just that I have so much to do in Puerto Deseado."

"Are you really complaining about being sent within thirty miles of one of the world's great natural wonders, all expenses paid?"

I had to smile. Castro was right. This trip meant spending twelve hours driving through the endless Santa Cruz flatlands instead of working on the case, but at least it was a good excuse to visit the glacier.

"So, you've never been to the *Ventisquero*?" I asked.

"Is that the same thing as the glacier?"

"Yes," I said, laughing. "That's what we call it in Patagonia, at least."

"Then no, I've never been to the *Ventisquero*," he answered, offering me the yerba mate gourd. I held the steering wheel with one hand and took the gourd with the other, keeping my eyes on the road, which stretched beyond the horizon.

The bitter infusion was exactly what I needed to ward off my post-lunch sluggishness. The water was at exactly the right temperature, and Castro had put in just a little bit of sugar, the way I like it. On a trip as long as that one, having someone who can prepare a good yerba mate is invaluable.

"You're going to love it," I said, taking another sip from the gourd. "There's a reason people come from all over the world to see it."

I put my hand back on the wheel and remembered my last trip to the Perito Moreno, three years earlier, with Aunt Susana. That glacier was like *The Godfather*: no matter how much people talked it up beforehand, the first time you saw it, it left you speechless.

"Yes, I'm sure I'll enjoy it. I've wanted to see it for some time now. Though my granddaughter will kill me when she finds out I went without her."

"You have a granddaughter?" I feigned. I'd read he had a granddaughter in the article about his son's death and seen photos of her on his Facebook profile.

"I do. Her name is Alicia. Six years old. She's a fanatic for anything having to do with forests, mountains, or glaciers."

"Really? Where'd she get that from? Did you ever take her to the mountains?"

"Never!" Castro laughed. "She sees it all on TV. She's glued to the screen whenever there's a shot of a snow-covered forest or a house in the woods with a smoking chimney. Much more so even than when she watches cartoons."

"Well, you'll have to bring her out here one day. Or at least take her to Mendoza or San Martín de los Andes—that's not as far from Buenos Aires."

"That would be brilliant," he said.

I briefly turned to hand back the gourd and saw that his gaze was lost in the endless road that lay ahead of us.

"Brilliant," he repeated. He was smiling, but his expression was melancholy, like he was picturing something very happy that was totally out of his reach.

CHAPTER 26

The next morning, half an hour after eating breakfast at the hotel, I parked in front of the address Menéndez-Azcuénaga had given us. His house was made of stone and wood and looked like the oldest building in the neighborhood by far.

Castro opened the wrought iron gate and made a chivalrous gesture that seemed to say *ladies first*, so I went in. We followed the cobblestone path over the meticulously cared-for lawn edged with marigolds. Such beautiful green grass would be practically unthinkable in Puerto Deseado, where you can only fill your water tank once every four days and where watering your front lawn is almost as frowned upon as lighting a cigarette with a hundred-peso bill.

The cobblestones stopped before a large double door made of walnut wood. I knocked using an old-fashioned bronze knocker. Then I saw a doorbell, so I rang, too, just in case.

When the door opened, I immediately recognized Sherlock from the hotel security footage. He was exactly as the men at La Preciosa had described him, with a tailored vest and a handlebar mustache that made him look like he was born fifty years too late.

"Good morning. I'm Detective Laura Badía, and this is the archaeologist Alberto Castro. We're from the court in Puerto Deseado. Are you Mr. Francisco Menéndez-Azcuénaga?"

The man smiled and used the tips of his fingers to briefly and feebly shake our hands. "That I am. Please, do come in. It is an honor to welcome you to my home. It is a special privilege, indeed, to receive the world's foremost scholar on Tehuelche lithic artifacts. Please do not take my praise as a slight against yourself, Miss Badía, but I am a true admirer of Dr. Castro's work in anthropology."

"Not at all," I answered, stepping into the house. It was warm and smelled like a wood-burning stove.

"Allow me to take your coats."

I nodded and removed my windbreaker, which he hung on a coatrack. The wooden cane I'd seen in the hotel security footage was resting in an umbrella stand on the floor. Castro, who had dressed for the South Pole, was ungracefully trying to balance his cardigan, scarf, and winter coat on two hooks.

"Thank you for seeing us, sir."

"The pleasure is all mine. It's not as if there are many demands upon my time. Come along, come in. Let's sit by the fireplace. Can I get you anything to drink? Tea? Coffee?"

I accepted his offer of coffee, and Castro asked for some chamomile tea. He gestured for us to wait a moment and walked down the hall.

"Wasn't he supposed to walk with a cane?" asked Castro.

I shrugged.

"I guess many older people only use it when they leave home," he said, answering his own question.

From the comfort of my armchair, I took in my surroundings. I had always dreamed of living in a house like that. A house from another time, with walls that were five feet thick and doors that would fit a giant. And a fireplace—another impossibility in Puerto Deseado. Burning firewood in the desert would cost a fortune.

Menéndez-Azcuénaga reemerged and sat facing me, next to a window through which I could see his garden.

"My housekeeper will bring the drinks shortly. You're quite lucky to have come when she's here—whenever I attempt to make coffee myself, it turns out vile."

I smiled but remained silent. Menéndez-Azcuénaga emptied the contents of his pipe into an ashtray on his chair's armrest. Then he lifted his head and looked me in the eyes.

"I had nothing to do with that man's death."

"You're referring to the murder of Julio Ortega in Puerto Deseado?"

He nodded. The trembling of his hands was amplified in his empty pipe, which he held by the mouthpiece.

"Did you know Ortega?"

"No, I've never seen him."

"But at the bar La Preciosa they told me . . ."

"I've never seen him in my life."

"I'm sure you'll understand, sir, that since you were seen over six hundred miles from your home, asking for a man on the night he was found dead, I'm going to have to press you for a more substantial explanation."

Menéndez-Azcuénaga let out a long sigh and nodded silently. Before speaking, he slowly refilled his pipe, then took a tool out of his pocket and compressed the tobacco.

"Will this be a bother?"

Castro and I both shook our heads, and he lit the tobacco with a lighter that made a sound like a small blowtorch.

"Let's start at the beginning," I said, lifting a hand. "How did you know Julio Ortega had that collection?"

"An old acquaintance who deals in antiques informed me over email. I'd prefer not to divulge his name, if that's at all possible."

"There's no need, we already know it. It's Ariel Ortiz, who's doing time at Pico Truncado—for illicit trade of cultural artifacts, incidentally."

Menéndez-Azcuénaga nodded in surprise. His expression said something along the lines of *If you already knew, why did you ask?*

"I haven't done anything illegal. I simply received an email from this individual, who, as you rightly pointed out, is currently serving out his sentence in a penitentiary."

"We're going to need those emails, sir."

The old man's face remained motionless for a second as he considered his response. He eventually gave several quick nods, but he didn't move from his chair.

"I'd gone to Puerto Deseado with a plan. I had hoped to find Ortega and to somehow get him to touch on the subject of arrowheads. I thought I would perhaps mention that I am a collector so that he might view me as a potential buyer. But it was essential that it appear casual. With deals such as these, there's no surer way of losing money than to appear desperate. Imagine if I'd presented myself before him and said, 'Hello, Mr. Ortega, my name is Francisco Menéndez-Azcuénaga, and I've traveled six hundred miles to purchase your arrowheads.' Why, I might as well write him a blank check."

"How did you know to look for him at La Preciosa?"

"My friend . . ."

"Ortiz, of course."

"That night, however, as I've no doubt you already know, Ortega didn't attend the poker game at La Preciosa," he continued. "I played several hands with his friends, initially hopeful that he may have been delayed, but as the hours passed, I became convinced he would not come."

"How late were you there?"

"Until around three in the morning, I'd imagine."

That coincided with the hotel security footage and the testimony I'd had a sub-officer get from the driver who took Menéndez-Azcuénaga back to the hotel.

"You may confirm this with the concierge at the Isla Pingüino Hotel, where I stayed that night. He was a tall boy, with quite large teeth."

I didn't tell him that I'd already talked to the hotel staff. But his confidence showed he knew they'd back up his alibi.

There were three possibilities: One, the old man was telling the truth. Two, the old man had come and gone from the hotel undetected. Three, the old man had bribed the receptionist to help him dodge the cameras. He didn't seem strapped for cash.

"I'd intended to return to La Preciosa the following evening, but as I was having my breakfast, I heard a report of the murder on the radio. I was gripped by panic. I, an unknown man from out of town, had just arrived in Puerto Deseado and inquired about Ortega, and only a few hours later, Ortega was found dead. Surely, you can imagine my alarm."

"So you decided to leave Puerto Deseado."

"What else was I to do? Remain and ask family members about the arrowheads at the man's funeral? Go to the police and say that, despite the extraordinary timing, I had no hand in any wrongdoing?"

"Okay, Mr. Menéndez-Azcuénaga, let's say you're telling the truth. You don't know anything about the murder. Then why are we here? What did you have us come for?"

"I don't know anything about who that man was, or how they killed him, or, indeed, who 'they' were. But I'm quite certain of their motive."

CHAPTER 27

"In my email to the court, I believe I made it quite clear that I wished to discuss the arrowheads that disappeared from the scene of the crime, Miss Badía," said Menéndez-Azcuénaga, leaning back in his chair after releasing a mouthful of smoke.

"How would you know what was and wasn't at the crime scene?"

"Well, it doesn't take a genius. One day, I learned that Julio Ortega had come into possession of most of the Panasiuk Collection, and I went to attempt to purchase it from him, but he wound up dead before I had the chance. Two days later, I saw the arrowheads for sale online."

He leaned over the table, grabbed a folder, and pulled out a copy of the same photograph we'd found on Ortega's phone.

"Sorry, two days later you saw them where?"

A devilish grin appeared on the old man's face, exposing countless wrinkles under both eyes. "See here, I am an impassioned collector of lithic art. It's in my blood. And although I personally discovered many of the pieces in my possession, I cannot deny that, from time to time, I may have purchased a piece of particular interest."

"I guess that explains your friendship with a crook like Ariel Ortiz."

"*Crook* is quite an ugly and extravagant word for him, but yes. And besides dealing with men like Ortiz, every day I visit a number of websites where every once in a blue moon, I find a piece that isn't so bad."

He avoided eye contact with Castro. I figured he knew, or could guess, the archaeologist's position on buying and selling cultural artifacts.

"It's seldom that anything new surfaces, and even rarer that you find a piece that's worth the trouble, but two days after Ortega's death, someone put these arrowheads up for sale," he said, pointing at the photo.

"We'll need the name of that website."

"Of course. It's called Mercado Fácil."

"You're telling me you can buy Tehuelche artifacts on the biggest online marketplace in the country?" I asked, astounded. I'd pictured this kind of contraband being bought and sold in dark, invitation-only corners of the internet with servers in Eastern Europe.

"Indeed, you would be surprised by the items for sale on Mercado Fácil. Though I must admit, I, too, was a bit surprised to see the collection there. I'd have sold such a collection on a specialized page, with a global presence. That was how I intuited that the seller was unaware of its true value."

"How much did it cost?"

"It was in auction mode. When I saw it, it had not yet received a single bid."

"Was there a photo?"

"Naturally."

"*This* photo?"

"No. Fortunately, I thought to download a copy. Please, have a look."

He took out another photo of the collection from the same brown folder. This one was taken from a different angle, with less light. The arrowheads were in the same red velvet display case but without the pane of glass. The fifth arrowhead was missing from the middle of the triangle— the one I knew was in my desk drawer, at the courthouse. The photo must have been taken after Ortega's death.

"Did you contact the seller?" I asked.

"I did. I asked to meet with him in person so that I might see the arrowheads for myself. I said I was interested, but he never responded. A few hours later, the post had been taken down."

"Do you remember the name of the seller?"

"No, but I do remember that he had no feedback from previous transactions."

"It must have been a new account, just to sell those arrowheads. Could you email me this picture?" I asked, pointing to the photo he had downloaded from the post.

"Of course, but first, I would be interested in knowing exactly what my role is in this case. Am I still a suspect?"

"Mr. Menéndez-Azcuénaga, this is an unofficial discussion. We came here because you said you had information for us. We're here to listen to what you have to say. Later, my staff and I will come to our own conclusions."

He nodded slowly, twisting his mustache. I didn't know how to interpret his half smile.

"And Dr. Castro is on your staff?"

"We've brought him in as a consultant on lithic art."

Lithic art. I'd used that term dozens of times over the past few days, but I'd never heard it before Ortega's death. For me, they'd always just been arrowheads.

"We understand that you have the largest private collection in the province," I said.

"The largest collection, indeed, public or private. I have over twelve thousand pieces. I believe the museum in Puerto Deseado holds the second-largest collection. They're a bit shy of ten thousand pieces. Would you like to see my collection?"

"We would love to, if it's not too much trouble," said Castro.

"How about you finish telling us what you know, and then you show us?" I said.

"An excellent proposition."

Just then, a stout fiftysomething woman emerged from the kitchen, carrying a tray with three cups and saucers.

"Thank you, Amalia," said Menéndez-Azcuénaga as the woman placed the coffees and Castro's chamomile tea on the table.

"What can you tell us about the Panasiuk Collection?" I asked.

"Plenty," he answered, "though perhaps Dr. Castro already knows most of the story."

"But I don't, so please tell us."

He nodded solemnly and sipped his coffee before speaking. "Teodor Panasiuk was a Polish immigrant who arrived in Argentina in the early 1920s. Many of the Europeans who migrated in that era earned a living doing farmwork, and Panasiuk was no exception. He wound up in Patagonia, at a ranch near Cardiel Lake. Have you ever visited Cardiel, Miss Badía?"

"No."

"Well, unless you happen to be a devoted trout fisherman, there is absolutely nothing to do there. The word *lake* conjures up images of trees and frondescence. Nothing could be further from the truth. Cardiel Lake is an enormous water mirror in the middle of nowhere. The lands surrounding it are as brown and desolate as the mesa anywhere else in the Santa Cruz Province. I'm telling you this so that you'll appreciate just how limited Teodor Panasiuk's potential hobbies really were."

"So he took to searching for arrowheads?" I ventured.

"Indeed. Though he also collected spearheads, scrapers, axes . . ."

I burned my tongue on the coffee Amalia had brought.

"You must understand, Miss Badía, that those of us with a fondness for arrow collecting do nothing by half measures. To the general population, the prospect of spending a day staring at the ground and digging up every sliver of stone that pokes through the dirt must sound torturous. But once one 'gets the bug,' as I did, and as Teodor did nearly a century ago, the search becomes a lifelong pursuit."

I remembered how Aunt Susana had proudly hung her best arrowheads on her dining room wall.

"Teodor Panasiuk would have been just another anonymous field hand with a hobby if he hadn't heard a story that changed his life. You see, in the twenties, there were still a few Tehuelche camps near Cardiel Lake. Mind you, they weren't ambushing unwitting guanacos with bows and arrows anymore. They were carrying rifles and riding horses by his time. Over the years, Panasiuk became close with these people and established genuine friendships with several Tehuelches, who were accustomed to white men—or *huincas*, as they called them—coming only to displace or subjugate them. He got on especially well with one of the women at the camp, who wore an iridescent arrowhead around her neck. She was the one who told him the legend of Yalen."

Menéndez-Azcuénaga lifted his cup and gestured at Castro to continue the story.

"I already told Laura that the legend makes no sense from an anthropological point of view," Castro said, turning to me. "They also say that whoever reunites all fifteen of Chief Yalen's iridescent arrowheads will become immortal, like the stones themselves."

"What matters is not whether a legend is real," said Menéndez-Azcuénaga, "but which legends we choose to believe, since our beliefs become our actions, and our actions are as real as can be. Certainly, Panasiuk's beliefs had a real effect on him: he spent twenty-five years searching for the iridescent arrowheads and eventually found fourteen of them."

"How did he do it?"

"Inquiry, research, and mainly money," said Menéndez-Azcuénaga. He lifted a finger, apparently to indicate that we should wait a moment. He disappeared through a door. A few minutes later, he returned with a plastic folder, which he opened in front of us.

It was full of yellowing pages from old regional newspapers. I picked one up, careful not to tear it. Between ads for mange treatments and fencing materials was a small box with thick lettering: *Seeking arrowheads crafted from iridescent stone. Good compensation.*

Beneath the ad was the number for a post office box in Gobernador Gregores.

"Panasiuk was entirely open about his obsession. He would tell anyone who would listen that he was prepared to pay handsomely for arrowheads made from iridescent stone."

"And people didn't try to dupe him?"

"Indeed they did, right and left. Remember that there is also opal in Patagonia, but unlike Amazonian opal, it is not considered a semiprecious stone. The iridescence of Patagonian opal is muted. It doesn't hold a candle to the stone brought from the Amazon, which literally casts its own rainbow. The Panasiuk arrowheads pull apart the light and release brighter, deeper colors than any other stone. Someone who has seen the genuine thing would never have difficulty identifying an imitation."

It was true. The arrowhead we'd found at Ortega's house and the one in the museum were like nothing I'd ever seen before.

"Panasiuk employed a very simple technique to shield himself from fraud: in the twenty-five years he spent collecting the arrowheads, never once did he show them to anyone. And so, no one knew exactly what he was looking for. If they brought him a true opal arrowhead from the Amazon, he would purchase it. If they brought something else, he would politely decline. And with this method he succeeded in collecting fourteen arrowheads."

"Weren't there supposed to be fifteen? What happened to the other one?"

"Aha! If you'd paid attention to the story, you would already have your answer."

"The fifteenth arrowhead was the one the Tehuelche woman was wearing around her neck when she told Panasiuk the story, twenty-five years earlier," interjected Castro, pointing to his own chest as if he were wearing the arrowhead.

"Quite right, Doctor," affirmed Menéndez-Azcuénaga. "And if you're to fully appreciate this story's denouement, I must explain that by this point, Teodor Panasiuk was no longer a poor immigrant who sheared someone else's sheep. In those twenty-five years, he had become one of the most important ranchers in the province, owner of six properties, and a shareholder in La Sociedad."

"La Sociedad is the biggest grocery store chain in Patagonia," I explained to Castro.

"And as is wont to happen when one succeeds in business, people began to talk. Some attributed Panasiuk's prosperity to the charm of the arrowheads he had collected. To this day, others maintain that he earned his fortune through shady dealings when he was president of the Gobernador Gregores Livestock Cooperative. But one way or another, he had become a wealthy man. Very wealthy. And so, he gave that Tehuelche woman a house in town in exchange for her necklace."

"He traded a house for an arrowhead?"

Menéndez-Azcuénaga shook his head with disappointment, as if I'd learned nothing. "He traded a house for *the* arrowhead. The piece he needed to complete the collection to which he'd dedicated all of twenty-five years."

"Yeah? And did he live forever after all, like the legend says?" I asked sarcastically.

Menéndez-Azcuénaga chuckled and twirled his gray mustache with his fingers. "He certainly did not. But I doubt Panasiuk would have believed the bit about immortality. For him, it was a personal obsession, a challenge. Some people run marathons, others collect arrowheads. For him, bringing together all fifteen arrowheads was worth more than a house in Gobernador Gregores. After all, what is a house to one of the richest men in Santa Cruz?"

"How do you know all this?"

Menéndez-Azcuénaga got up from his chair and motioned for us to follow him.

"I know it because Teodor Panasiuk was my grandfather," he said wryly.

CHAPTER 28

We followed Menéndez-Azcuénaga down a hallway and through the kitchen, where Amalia was washing dishes with her back to us. We stopped in front of another tall wooden door.

"Welcome to my own little Treasure Island," he said with exaggerated extravagance.

We stepped into a rectangular room. It was larger than the room where we had just been sitting, and the walls were covered with cases of arrowheads, spears, and broken Tehuelche pottery.

"You found all these yourself?" asked Castro, scanning each of the walls.

"Not all of them. I inherited several from my family."

"From Teodor Panasiuk?" I asked.

"No, he left his entire collection to the museum in Gobernador Gregores. Well, nearly his entire collection."

At one end of the room was a wooden desk covered in books and papers, and behind it was a leather-backed chair that, like the house's doors, was tall enough for a giant. Menéndez-Azcuénaga pushed aside the papers so that the only thing on the desk was one of those rectangular leather pads. He looked at us for an instant, smiled, then lifted the leather pad, revealing a glass case set into the polished wood. Then he flipped a switch near his knees, and the compartment was lit from all four sides. Castro and I looked inside, incredulous.

Beneath the glass were fifteen arrowheads, arranged in a triangle, exactly like the diagram Castro had shown me a few days earlier. But they weren't iridescent. They were gold.

"The Fonseca Diagram," I said.

"What is this?" asked Castro.

"As I said, the iridescent arrowheads were extremely important to Teodor. So much so that he had a replica of each one cast in solid twenty-four-karat gold. They were the only things he didn't donate to the museum."

"They must be worth a fortune."

"Not as much as the real thing, Miss Badía."

"But what happened to the real collection?"

"That is something no one knows. When he was eighty, Teodor agreed, for the first time in his life, to have the collection displayed at the museum in Río Gallegos. People were to come from every corner of Argentina to study it. Legend or no legend, they are the only Tehuelche arrowheads known to have been carved from Amazonian opal. It was a beautiful collection of incalculable archaeological importance."

"The way you're talking, I'm guessing the exhibition never happened?"

"The day before the collection was to be brought to Río Gallegos, two masked men broke into Teodor's house in Gobernador Gregores. They beat him, tied him up, and took the collection."

"Hang on a second, there's something I don't get. If they took all fifteen pieces from Panasiuk's house, how did thirteen end up with Ortega, one with the museum in Puerto Deseado, and one in a private collection?" I asked.

The collector shrugged. "My only hypothesis is that the new owner was forced to sell some of the arrowheads. Out of economic necessity, perhaps."

"Yeah. I'm not sure I buy that."

"If I'm being sincere with you, Miss Badía, I'm not sure I do, either. All of this is mere speculation. Regardless, the arrowheads didn't surface for decades. I've spent my whole life monitoring the black market, and until eight days ago, I hadn't seen a trace of them."

"I'm guessing you haven't seen anything else about them online in the past week?"

"Nothing at all. And I've spent hours on end clicking refresh."

"You still plan to buy the collection, even after all this?" asked Castro, incensed.

"No, I don't believe that will be necessary."

"What do you mean?"

"I am Teodor Panasiuk's only living heir. Letting you find the arrowheads and bring them to me seems far more convenient."

CHAPTER 29

Menéndez-Azcuénaga invited us to have lunch with him, but I thought it would be better to decline. Everything seemed to suggest he was innocent, but it still felt unwise to stay and socialize with a person of interest.

We didn't have time to drive back to Puerto Deseado that day, so Castro and I decided to use our free afternoon to visit the glacier. We bought a couple of exorbitantly overpriced sandwiches at a store in Calafate and ate them on the way to the Perito Moreno.

Thirty miles of flatlands later, long after the sandwiches had been devoured, I cruised to a stop at the entrance to Los Glaciares National Park. A ranger in a brown uniform stepped out of a small stone building with a ticket book in her hand. A sign to our right informed us that Castro—a nonresident of the province—would pay twice as much as me to enter the park. Foreigners had to pay ten times as much.

"Did something happen?" she asked, leaning down to talk to me through the window.

"Sorry?" I asked.

"We don't usually get police here."

I remembered we were in one of the precinct's vehicles, not in my car.

"We came from Puerto Deseado on work, but we have the afternoon free."

"Uh-huh. Straight ahead, then. Enjoy the park."

"You're not going to charge us?"

The woman smiled, stood up straight, and gestured for us to drive forward.

◆ ◆ ◆

The landscape changed almost the instant we entered the park. We left the monotonous brown plains behind us and entered a forest, zigzagging between lenga and *ñire* trees and skirting a lake full of ice chunks. I was sure anyone who had made that drive would understand why I fantasized (along with many others) of leaving everything and going to live in the mountains.

After a few minutes of silence, I looked at Castro. He was leaning his head against the headrest and staring at the car ceiling.

"Are you okay? You're pale."

"It's the curvy road," he said, wiping a few drops of sweat from his forehead.

"You want me to pull over?"

"No, if you could just go a little slower that would be fine."

"Here, let's stop at the lookout," I said. A sign said it was half a mile to the "Curva de los Suspiros," the final bend in the road before the glacier comes into view.

Castro nodded, put on a hat with earflaps, and rolled down the window for some air.

The glacier came into view as we rounded the famous curve. I slowed down, turned left, and parked at a lookout with no guardrail. Castro wound a scarf around his neck and opened the door before I turned off the engine. He threw up next to the rear bumper.

"I'm fine," he said, coughing. "I just don't do well with winding roads."

I brought him a tissue and a bottle of water. After he recovered, he hung a camera around his neck, and together we walked to the lookout, our eyes glued to the huge mass of ice that ascended with the mountains and got lost in the clouds.

"They certainly gave this curve the right name," said Castro, removing the camera's lens cap. I nodded, but he didn't see because he was already snapping away, the camera pressed against his face.

I leaned on the car hood and looked at the *Ventisquero*, smiling as I thought about the local name for the glacier. I was sure that any tourist who used it at the entrance would be charged the resident rate without having to show ID. My skin tingled under my windbreaker—I was totally overcome with a sense of pride for belonging to such a beautiful place.

We got back in the car and drove the remaining six miles to the parking lot at the slowest speed possible. From there, we walked to the observation decks facing the glacier.

"It's incredible," said Castro, supporting himself on the wooden railing.

The glacier ended in a three-mile-long wall—blue and white, like the flag of Argentina. It rose twenty stories above the lake. Dozens of irregularly shaped ice floes drifted on the surface of the water.

"Listen," I said, putting a finger to my lips. The silence was perfect except for the wind and the distant murmuring of German tourists.

"So peaceful," said Castro, but I gestured for him to remain silent. That was when we heard the first rumble.

"Was that thunder?" Castro asked, looking at the crystal-clear sky.

"It's the ice breaking," I said, laughing. "The snow falling in the mountains is constantly pushing the glacier forward, so the ice cracks and breaks apart. It's one of the few glaciers in the world that isn't receding."

"I suppose we can count ourselves lucky if we see a piece fall?"

"Very lucky."

"It's unbelievable," said Castro. "A friend of mine was in New Zealand a while back, and she told me that all the glaciers there are big tourist attractions, too, but that they're melting at an alarming rate. She showed me a photo of the glacier today and one from the sixties, and the difference broke my heart."

"That's not the case with the Perito Moreno, fortunately. It's always moving forward, so it makes sense that it continues to crack. Look, that piece looks like it's close to falling," I said, pointing to a truck-sized chunk of ice protruding from the glacier wall. It was surrounded by a crack, and it looked like it would topple if a bird landed on it.

We stood there in silence for a while, watching the ice and listening to its loud creaking and crunching, but my piece never fell, and neither did any other. Not that we could see, anyway. We sat drinking yerba mate, almost wordlessly. Castro's face was glued to his camera, which he used to take at least fifteen thousand photos.

"I read somewhere that the glacier is bigger than Buenos Aires."

"Probably a smaller population, though," said Castro, and we laughed.

"When I was a little girl, I always wanted to be a park ranger. Just to be alone with nature."

"I could never do that," said Castro. "I'm a city person. I love traveling the country doing fieldwork, but I enjoy it much more knowing I have a return ticket to Buenos Aires."

"I wouldn't go back to Buenos Aires if you paid me. My college years there were plenty."

"Well, if you could go anywhere in the world, where would it be?" he asked.

"Somewhere with lots and lots of water. Someplace green."

"Here, maybe?"

I laughed. "Maybe, but I'd rather be a little farther north, where I wouldn't get snowed in half the year. I think the perfect place for me would be somewhere between Chubut and Neuquén, but far from the touristy areas. I don't want anything to do with Bolsón or Bariloche."

"Not a bad choice. You picked the most beautiful non-tourist destination there is."

"I mean, if you're going to dream, you might as well dream big, right?"

"At least you'll never have trouble finding work. There are murders to investigate everywhere you go."

"Yeah, but I think I'd change jobs if I went somewhere like that."

"Really? What would you want to do?"

That was my problem. No matter how hard I tried, I could never picture myself in any other line of work.

"Maybe photography," I improvised. "Lend me your camera for a second?"

He gave it to me. I took two steps back and put him in the frame.

"All right, smile—let's take a photo you can show your granddaughter."

When I said that, Castro smiled, and I took the photo. But as soon as I put down the camera, that same bittersweet expression from the day before returned to his eyes. He thanked me for the photo, then turned and leaned against the railing.

I thought the image of a gray-haired man looking out at the Perito Moreno with his back to the photographer was pretty, so I took a few more shots.

"Okay, I don't think you need to take any more," he said brusquely, without turning to face me.

I went over to the railing and leaned against it.

"Sorry—I didn't think it would bother you," I said, giving back the camera.

"It's not a problem. I just don't like being in photos very much."

We fell silent. A few small birds flew over the lake, which separated us from the ice. I wished a piece of the glacier—mine or any other—would fall so we could talk about something else, but all of the cracking sounds seemed to come from inside the glacier.

"I don't see my granddaughter much," he said before long.

I couldn't decide if I should ask him why or if I should bring up literally any other subject. In the end, I kept my mouth shut.

"My son, Lautaro, passed away when she was a baby, and I don't have a very good relationship with her mother. She doesn't let me see her often."

That explained the melancholy looks.

I felt dirty for having read that article about his son's death, and I almost wanted to tell him about it so I could apologize. It felt like I'd spied on him. Part of me also wanted to hug him so he could finally let out all the tears that were audibly stuck in his throat.

I was about to put a hand on his shoulder when we heard another rumble, much louder than before, and an enormous mass of ice sank into the water, almost in slow motion. Everyone on the observation deck, including us, cried out in astonishment. After crashing into the water, the mass reemerged on the surface, now by far the largest of the ice floes. Before the murmur from the tourists diminished, another huge piece, the size of a basketball court, fell from the upper face of the glacier.

Castro and I whooped again, along with the other tourists. When I turned to Castro, I saw that he had tears in his eyes. I rested my head on one of his shoulders and my hand on the other.

Out of the corner of my eye, I looked at the piece I'd pointed out, the one that had seemed the most tenuous. It hadn't budged.

CHAPTER 30

The trip to Puerto Deseado was easy, and Castro didn't bring his grand-daughter back up. I had been up late the night before: when I got back to my hotel room, I called Echeverría to fill her in on everything Teodor Panasiuk's grandson had told us. I also asked her to file a court order that would compel Mercado Fácil to hand over information on the ad for the arrowheads. The photo Menéndez-Azcuénaga had downloaded and the publication date would be enough for them to find it in their database. Echeverría told me to leave it to her and urged us to drive carefully.

I got home around nine at night, took a shower, and went straight to bed. When I woke up at six thirty in the morning, it was still dark.

I drank a cup of tea with milk, put on a long goose-down coat Aunt Susana had given me, and stepped into the winter morning. Miraculously, my Corsa started on the first try, but the windshield wipers barely put a dent in the frost that had fallen overnight. I felt around under the seat until I found the yellow plastic scraper. Tucking my chin as deep in my coat as I could, I scraped a rectangle in the ice on the front and back windshields. I was at least able to see well enough to make it to the courthouse.

Debarnot, the sub-officer who'd found Julio's body, opened the door for me at the courthouse. I asked him how the night shift had been, then walked to my lab through the building's still-dark hallways.

I turned on my computer. Between newsletters and official bulletins, one email in particular caught my eye. It had the subject line "DNA ANALYSIS RESULTS."

The body of the email was empty, but there was a PDF attached. I recognized the official letterhead of the Regional Forensics Laboratory in Río Gallegos. I skipped the bullshit and went straight to the results:

> Following an analysis of genetic similarities, we conclude with 99.99999% certainty that the confirmed sample (saliva) and the unconfirmed sample (blood) belong to the same individual.

I picked up the phone and called Lamuedra.

"It must have gone well in Calafate for you to be calling me so early."

I was surprised to hear his voice sound so normal, like he'd been awake for hours.

"No. Well, yes. But I'm calling about something else. You're not going to like it."

"Christ, what now?"

"I ordered a DNA test to compare the drop of A-negative blood we found in Ortega's house with a suspect's saliva."

"Since when do we have a suspect?"

"It was a hunch, Commissioner. I didn't have any evidence to justify the test."

"You . . . tested someone's DNA without their consent and without any evidence against them?"

"But that's not the most important thing right now, Commissioner. The important thing is that I know whose blood we found in Julio Ortega's house."

There were a few seconds of silence on the other end of the line.

"Where are you?" he asked.

"At the courthouse."

"Don't leave."

◆ ◆ ◆

Ten minutes later, Lamuedra stormed into the lab and slammed the door.

"Who the fuck do you think you are, Badía? Wonder Woman? We put you in charge of this investigation so you'd do it right. There are laws in this country. You can't just gallivant around doing whatever tickles your oyster. Do I have to remind you that you're a goddamn cop?"

"Of course, Commissioner, you're absolutely right, I'm sorry. But the important thing right now—"

"The important thing right now and always is to do things right," he interrupted. "So you'd better fill me in on this colossal turd of a situation you've gotten us into so we can try and fix it."

So I did. There was no need to tell him who Enrique Vera was, but I did have to explain why I suspected him. I also described how I had gotten the Coke can with his saliva and fingerprints.

I wrapped up my speech: "Commissioner, Vera has no idea we did the test. But now we know he killed Ortega. We can go to his house and say someone reported him anonymously, then see if he talks."

"Uh-huh. So now, on top of doing an illegal DNA test, you want to fabricate a police report?"

I took a deep breath and told myself to count to ten before speaking. Talking back to any superior in the heat of the moment was never a good idea, and Lamuedra wasn't just any higher-up, he was the commissioner. I got to seven before I opened my mouth.

"Look, somebody committed this atrocity in Puerto Deseado. We know exactly who he is and where we can find him. What do you want to do? Sit around here, filling out your precious little forms while a known murderer walks around town, footloose and fancy-free? Doesn't it make more sense to go ask him where he was that night, so that, if nothing else, he knows someone's got eyes on him?"

Lamuedra let out a long breath, trying to calm down.

"Show me the results," he said.

When he finished reading, he looked at me severely and shook his head.

"You're going to get yourself into a real nasty situation one day, Badía. Let's go."

"Where?"

"To talk to Vera."

CHAPTER 31

The police pickup truck's blue headlights reflected against the front of Enrique Vera's house. The sun had technically risen, but at eight thirty in the morning in a town as far south as Puerto Deseado, light was still scarce. I could smell low tide when I opened the truck door.

On the other side of a tall gate, Vera's green car was parked beside his house. All the lights were off. The casino was open until four thirty. As far as I knew, Vera always stayed until closing time, since that was when he got his most desperate clients. He would only have gotten a few hours of sleep at that point.

I rang the bell next to the gate and heard it ring inside the house. I counted to twenty before ringing again. Then to ten, then again. No response.

I pulled the gate's ice-cold latch, which opened freely. Lamuedra took a few long strides to the door and knocked with a closed fist. I thought I heard something, so I put my ear to the door. Lamuedra started looking around the outside of the house.

"There he is," he said softly, pointing behind Vera's green car.

I walked to where Lamuedra was standing and saw Enrique's bulky figure climbing the wall behind the house. I started to run after him, but Lamuedra grabbed me forcefully by the arm.

"What are you doing?" I whispered.

Without a word, he pointed with his chin to the space between the house and Vera's car. I heard a hoarse growl and, in the blue dawn light, saw the silhouette of a huge Argentinian mastiff. Before it started barking, it made a point of showing us its long, perfectly white teeth.

My muscles froze and my lungs closed up. I had a pathological fear of dogs.

"Run, Laura," Lamuedra said behind me, aiming at the animal with his Browning.

I clung as close to the wall as I could.

"Get out of here! Fuck, get *out*," cried Lamuedra, but the mastiff only growled louder. Then it ran toward us.

The shot reverberated around the property, shattering the morning calm. I heard several sharp whimpers, and the dog fled to a wooden doghouse on the other side of the property, tail between its legs.

"Let's go, quick. I missed. I don't know how long before he gets over the shock and the pain in his ears."

I ran to the wall Vera had climbed, jumped, and gripped the top with my hands. Ignoring the cement scratching my palms, I felt around with my feet until I found a gap between bricks. My other foot was still feeling for a hold when something grabbed it and pulled hard. Lamuedra was guiding my foot to his shoulder.

"Follow him. I'll be behind in the truck," he said.

I nodded and pulled myself to the top of the wall. On the other side was a dirt ledge no wider than a few feet with a ravine flowing beneath it. I saw Vera in the ravine, running on the garbage and rubble that lined both sides of the water. In the distance, past the end of the lagoon, I could faintly see a narrow space between two large stone slopes.

"He's heading for the gorge!" I yelled before climbing down.

I stepped onto the embankment. It was at least thirty feet down to the ravine, at a nearly ninety-degree angle. But I knew it must be possible to get down uninjured—the proof of it was running away at full speed, a soccer field's length ahead of me.

I put one foot on the slope. The earth underneath gave way, I lost my balance, and in an attempt not to tumble forward, I instead fell on my ass. With no control over what was happening, I sped down the slope until my feet abruptly slammed against the ground and the impact whipped up my legs and spine. At first I couldn't move, but the gravel around me continued to fall in a mini-avalanche. I sat up and ran after Vera, who had already reached the lampposts surrounding the lagoon. He was closing in on the gorge.

The rocks in my shoes made it hard to reduce the distance between me and Vera. Not to mention that he ran fast—he had legs the size of tree trunks, after all. I came to a large field and tried to gain as much ground as I could on the flat terrain, but Vera got lost in a cluster of makeshift shelters. From there, all he'd have to do was cross a street and enter the gorge.

The beam of the police truck's headlights appeared behind a hill and stopped where Vera had just crossed. I kept running and saw Lamuedra's silhouette get out and start running. I lost sight of him among the rocks.

Without slowing down, I drew my pistol and entered the gorge, which hadn't yet been infiltrated by the weak morning light.

"Laura!" I heard Lamuedra cry. I ran faster.

I scanned the ochre rocks for the commissioner, but it took a few seconds for me to see him behind a curve. He was holding his Browning with both hands, pointing it slightly downward.

"He got away from me," he said. He collapsed on the ground, breathing fast.

"If he climbs the gorge walls, he'll end up where they're building those new developments," I said. I called the station and told them to send a patrol car to help us look for him. "You go in the truck," I told Lamuedra. "I'll follow him through the gorge on foot."

"Be careful," Lamuedra said, forcing himself up and into the truck.

"Don't worry," I said, gesturing at my gun.

CHAPTER 32

The gorge was a wide crack in Puerto Deseado's irregular cliffs, formed by centuries of scarce rain and unrelenting wind. The surrounding areas were uninhabited—people were reluctant to build that high in the rocks, where it was so windy and the terrain was so uneven. I looked up. I knew there were houses near there, but from where I stood, all I could see were the gorge's irregular walls and some red-bellied clouds lit from below by the rising sun.

I ran until the black earth and fertile soil gave way to a very steep rock slope. Had Vera really climbed that? Or was he hiding in one of the hundreds of nooks and crannies in the volcanic rock?

I heard a small rock fall from above me.

I climbed up to a huge boulder, which seemed to have become dislodged from the precipice at some point only to get stuck halfway down. As soon as I managed to climb around it, Enrique Vera pounced. My head struck a rock, making me bite down on my tongue. My mouth filled with the metallic taste of blood.

"I don't want to hit a woman," he said.

My pistol was no longer in my right hand.

Vera shook me by the shoulders, then tried to run off through the rocks, but I heaved myself toward him and grabbed his ankles. He fell forward, and we both rolled a few feet down until we hit a precipice in the stone. Both of our faces were in the dirt.

I clutched his feet to my chest. My gun was about four feet away. I stretched to grab it, but as soon as I moved my arm, Vera wrestled his legs free and used his heel to strike my nose with the force of an angry bull. I brought my hands to my face. Warm blood oozed between my fingers. I had to blink several times before my vision came back into focus, and by then, Vera was already scaling the rocks in front of me.

I grasped around until I felt the cold metal of my Browning. Vera was less than fifty feet in front of me, trying to climb a steep wall.

I wiped the tears from my eyes and aimed at his wide back, holding the gun in both hands. The wall was steep, and he was barely moving. I had a clear shot. It would be like killing a cockroach with insecticide. I disengaged the safety. My rage, the adrenaline, and the blood gushing from my nose all urged me to put a bullet in his muscular back. My head, being more rational, reminded me that a shot to the leg would be enough to stop him. And my police training told me I better not so much as *think* of pulling the trigger on an unarmed, unaccused man with his back to me. It would have been the end of my career.

"Don't go any farther or I'll shoot," I cried, but Vera had already found a foothold and was easily scaling the rock.

By the time I repeated my warning, he was over the top and running away at full speed.

CHAPTER 33

It was below freezing in Puerto Deseado the next day, and the dark gray sky plastered the town in a thick layer of slush. I parked in the museum's nearly empty parking lot and got out of the car, keeping a tight hold on the door so it wouldn't sweep open in the wind. The radio said gusts might reach seventy-five miles an hour.

Before going inside, I turned my face against the wind, closed my eyes, and breathed in deep. The thick raindrops falling on my inflamed nose and the cold air flowing through my nostrils numbed my face a little, giving me an instant of relief.

At the hospital, they had said my septum wasn't damaged and that I just needed to wait for the swelling to go down. It had been twenty-four hours since Vera busted my nose with a kick, and it hurt more than ever. Worst of all, there wasn't a trace of Vera. We'd lost his trail completely.

And now this.

Just inside the museum, the director was waiting for me. A handful of employees were standing around, doing nothing. Arrowheads and broken glass lay on top of the white wood.

"Hi, Laura," said Virginia, kissing me on the cheek. "What happened to your face?"

"Nothing serious," I answered, taking out my camera to photograph the broken display case.

Unprompted, Virginia began explaining the scene. "I got here half an hour ago, fifteen minutes before we open, like I do every day. The first thing I saw was this shattered display. I think only one arrowhead is missing."

"Did they break anything else or move anything?"

"That window. That's where they came in," she said.

From the dents in the metal, it looked like the window had been forced open with a crowbar. It was closed, but rain was still seeping through the frame and dripping down the wall, gathering with it the dust that had accumulated since the last time it rained, months ago.

"It was open when I got here," Virginia continued. "I know you're not supposed to touch anything when this sort of thing happens, but I had to close it because water was pouring in."

"You don't have a security guard at night?" I asked, taking in the scene.

"We do. Pocho is the municipal employee who handles our night watch. But he doesn't work on weekends."

I wanted to tell Virginia how totally moronic it was not to have a security guard on the two nights of the week when this kind of thing was most likely to happen, but then I remembered the sign on the door, which informed potential visitors that the museum was open from eight in the morning to three in the afternoon from Monday to Friday, and from three to six on Saturdays. The museum wasn't so much a tourist attraction as a municipal agency.

"Do you know which arrowhead they took?"

"Yes, it's a very rare one. Maybe the rarest in the collection. It's made with this iridescent opal from . . ."

"From the Amazon," I said, taking more photos of the broken glass. "It's the one I came to see with Castro the other day."

"Exactly." Virginia nodded, a little astonished. "It makes sense that they would steal that one. It must be worth hundreds of dollars on the black market."

"Sorry, how much?"

"Oh, I don't know. Five hundred, if not more."

I remembered my conversation with Ariel Ortiz in his prison cell and saw that Virginia Lacar, director of the Mario Brozoski Museum, had no idea how much the stolen arrowhead was really worth.

"It's odd that they took only that one," she added. "Why not take all the arrowheads in this case? Why wouldn't they break into other cases? Some of these other arrowheads must be worth something, too. That wasn't the only rare piece here."

"Did you check the rest of the museum to see if anything else was missing?" I asked, looking toward the hall where they kept the artifacts recovered from the HMS *Swift*.

She gave me a funny look. "We only have two halls, this one and the one for the *Swift*. Nothing else is missing from either one."

"What about that back room?" I said, pointing toward the little workroom that Castro had taken me to when we'd visited.

Virginia apparently hadn't thought of that, because as soon as I mentioned it, she trotted off to her office. From the hall of lithic art, I could see her opening her desk drawer and moving objects around.

"Did someone take the key to the back room?" she asked out loud. The employees looked at one another and collectively shrugged.

Without waiting for Virginia, I went to the door behind the old printing press from *El Orden* and tried the doorknob. It was unlocked.

The first two tables, which held submerged artifacts recovered from the *Swift*, were still there. But the third table, the one Castro worked at, was pushed out of place, and several arrowheads were strewn on top of it. There were also some stone fragments on the floor. The dentist-style lamp was still on, bent straight up at a tight angle.

"It was ope—oh my God. What happened here?" Virginia asked when she came in and saw the room in disarray.

"It looks like there was a struggle."

She put her hands to her head and took in the small room. Her eyes stopped at a large metal storage cabinet, the standard-issue kind they have at public institutions.

"No wonder I couldn't find them." She pointed to the center of the cabinet: her key ring was hanging from the handle.

"Who else knows you keep those keys in your desk drawer?"

"The staff. Oh, and the archaeologists who work with us. But the only one in town right now is Castro."

"When was the last time Castro . . . ?"

I was interrupted by a metallic banging sound.

"What was that?" asked Virginia.

We heard it again. It was coming from the cabinet.

"What do you keep in there?" I asked.

"Tools and smocks for the restorers."

There was another, stronger bang from within the cabinet, making the door shake a little. Virginia took several steps back.

I carefully approached the cabinet and put a hand on the small key. The vibration from the fourth bang traveled through the handle and into my body, forming goose bumps on my arms. I turned the key, pulled on the handle, and instinctively jumped backward.

A wave of hot moisture came out the open cabinet door, and a few smocks on hangers shook forcefully. Alberto Castro was sitting on the bottom of the cabinet with a strip of silver tape over his mouth. There were tears in his eyes, and his wrists and ankles were tied with the same silver tape.

"Call the police station," I told Virginia.

CHAPTER 34

Virginia ran off to find a phone, and I cut Castro free using a needle I found on one of the worktables. He groaned when I tore the strip of tape off his mouth. Several white hairs from his beard came off with it.

"Thank you! I couldn't breathe in there."

"What happened?" I asked.

Virginia came back in, cell phone in hand. "The police are on their way."

Castro sat on a plastic chair next to the cabinet and tilted his head back, resting it on the cabinet he had been imprisoned in just moments earlier.

"They came in the window," he said, coughing.

"Who?" Virginia asked.

Castro gave her a scornful look.

"I don't know *who*. I was here working," he said, gesturing to the table. The light above it was still on. "I was classifying pieces from the latest campaign when I heard a noise. I shouted 'Who's there?' but no one responded. After a minute, I convinced myself that it had just been the wind or a cat and continued working. A few minutes later, someone grabbed me from behind and pulled me from my chair."

He squeezed his neck between his forearm and bicep to demonstrate how they had attacked him.

"I must have kicked around quite a bit before I passed out," he said with a faint smile, pointing to the twisted lamp and scattered arrowheads. "When I came to, I had tape on my mouth and my hands were tied."

"It was just one person?" I asked.

He nodded. "A man. He was . . ." Before he could finish, he was overtaken by a fit of hoarse coughs, the kind that hurt your lungs just to listen to.

"Are you okay? Was it very cold in there?"

"I'm fine. I've had a cold ever since our trip to Calafate." He coughed again and his face contorted in pain.

"As I was saying, it was a man," he continued. "He told me not to worry. He said that he wasn't going to hurt me, that he just wanted me to show him which arrowhead was from the Panasiuk Collection."

"What did he look like?"

"I don't know. He was wearing a gray ski mask with black trim around the eyes."

"Height? Was he fat, skinny? What did his voice sound like?"

"I don't remember very well. He choked me from behind. When I woke up and he spoke to me, he'd turned off nearly all the lights. He was certainly very strong. My throat still hurts." He gently massaged his neck as he spoke. "His voice struck me as excessively husky. I think he made it that way deliberately so I wouldn't recognize it."

"So you probably know him," concluded Virginia.

Castro shook his head. "I don't know anyone capable of something like this. He was a violent man. There was an expression in his eyes that I've never seen before. He was cold, like someone used to giving orders."

"What color were his eyes?"

Castro considered the question for a second. "I don't remember."

Great, that's helpful, I thought.

"Do you mean to tell me that there's been a piece from the Panasiuk Collection here all this time?" Virginia asked, indignant.

Castro took several deep breaths with his eyes closed, trying to calm down.

"Yes" was all he said.

"Then why didn't you say anything? Don't you think the museum staff ought to know about something like that?"

"Every one of you should have known!" roared Castro. "It was clearly labeled as allochthonous opal. Al-loch-tho-nous. Perhaps if this museum employed anyone besides a handpicked coterie of municipal employees who don't do anything but sit around drinking yerba mate, maybe someone, a single goddamn person, would know that *alloch*thonous means the opposite of *autoch*thonous. That is, the rock originated at a distance from its present position."

"And maybe if every archaeologist that came here wasn't some grandiose egomaniac from Buenos Aires, they would deign to explain to us lowly municipal employees just what we have in our museum. But no, his eminence Dr. Castro descends upon us from the capital, and we, the rustic Patagonians, must pay him reverence and even serve him his fucking yerba mate. You know what, asshole? I wish you'd been stuck in there for another day."

Virginia turned around and stormed out of the room, slamming the door behind her.

"We've never had a good relationship," Castro said, in case I'd missed that.

I just nodded and tried to change the subject. "How could the thieves have known the arrowhead was in the museum?"

"I had shared that fact with very few people until last year, when I published an article on the archaeological importance of the Panasiuk Collection in an academic journal. That article mentioned that there were two arrowheads made with Amazonian opal in Puerto Deseado. Though I didn't say exactly where they were, in order to prevent precisely the sort of thing that just happened."

"Considering you do work for this museum and that the collection here is huge, it must not have been hard for the thief to put two and two together. Do you have any idea who might have read that article?"

Castro shook his head. "Thousands of people read every paper I publish. Remember that I'm the leading authority on Tehuelche lithic art in the world."

His tone was serious and pragmatic, without a trace of pride or false humility. He was just a scholar stating a fact.

"Where's the other one?"

"The other what?"

"The other arrowhead from the Panasiuk Collection. The day we met, you said one was here and the other was in a private collection at some ranch."

"I promised the owners that I wouldn't reveal their identity if they let me study the arrowhead."

"Well, now their identity is part of a judicial investigation."

Castro gave me a wary look. We heard a police siren in the distance.

"It's in a small museum at Atardecer Ranch, a property across the estuary where people go to camp. The owners are very kind people. Whenever I visit Puerto Deseado, I spend several days working there."

I was about to write down the name of the ranch when I felt my phone vibrating in my pocket.

"Hello?"

"Can I talk to Miss Laura Badía?"

"That's me."

"Hi, Laura, it's Jorge Frau."

Just what I needed. A journalist.

"Hi, Jorge, what can I do for you?"

"I have information that may be useful in the Julio Ortega case."

"Wonderful. Come down to the station and file a report."

"No. I can only share this information with you. I'm going to ask you for a little something in return, obviously."

The line was silent for a second as I considered which was preferable: telling him to fuck off or threatening to have him arrested.

"Jorge, I don't know if you're aware, but if you know something about the murder and you don't tell me, that's obstructing justice. I wouldn't risk it, if I were you."

"I think you're the one who should avoid taking risks."

"What are you talking about?" I asked, taking a few steps away from Castro.

"Listen, Laura, I want to write about the case, not about the relationship between the victim and the girl leading the investigation. What'll it cost you? We'll sit down, have a coffee, answer a few questions. Nothing specific, nothing compromising."

"Absolutely not."

"All right, you're in charge. But whether you talk to me or not, tomorrow there's going to be a front-page report on the Ortega case in *El Orden*."

I looked out the window while I thought about what to say. It was starting to rain harder.

CHAPTER 35

The office and presses of *El Orden*, Puerto Deseado's only newspaper, were headquartered at the home of Jorge Frau, the weekly's owner, editor in chief, and sole reporter. I parked my Corsa out front, pulled up the hood of my windbreaker, and ran to the door. I took refuge under the tile eaves above the front door, which were pretty useless considering the rain was blowing sideways.

It took me a second to recognize the man who opened the door. It wasn't the Frau I knew. The man who greeted me with a kiss on the cheek was still unibrowed and unshaven, but he was also at least a hundred pounds lighter than I'd remembered.

"You haven't seen me since the operation, huh?" he asked, closing the door behind me.

I shook my head. I'd seen other people before and after gastric bypass surgery, but it was still weird to see someone who had gone to Buenos Aires to get their stomach reduced and now weighed half what they used to.

"Come on, let's go to my office," he said. Apparently, going to his office required walking through his cluttered, greasy-looking kitchen.

Frau opened the door that connected his house with the garage, where dozens of framed newspapers hung on the walls. Some were yellow, with freehand illustrations. Others had the current layout, which was smaller and on white paper. In the middle of the garage were two washing machine–sized printers and several stacks of A4 paper. Two newspaper pages would eventually be printed on both sides of each sheet.

On the back wall, flanked by ceiling-high shelves full of books and magazines, a vertically oriented computer monitor peeked out over the papers on Frau's desk. A Word document was open. He walked to his desk and offered me the swivel chair with a padded backrest from which I assumed he wrote, formatted, and printed the paper. He went to a corner, cleared another old chair, sat down, and used his feet to propel himself toward me. We sat face-to-face, with a small table covered in toner and test prints between us.

"Sweet of you to come here. It wouldn't have been a problem for me to meet you at the courthouse," he said.

No, the problem would have been me being seen with him. From then on, I would have been the first person everyone demanded an explanation from whenever he published anything unsavory in his paper.

Frau leaned back in his chair, rocking a little. He smiled before he started talking, creases appearing on his cheeks.

"So, Ortega really had the Panasiuk Collection and they killed him for it?"

"I can't answer that."

"I've got to write about something, don't I?" he insisted, leaning on the table between us.

"Yeah, you insinuated something like that over the phone. Why don't you cut the crap and tell me what you want?"

"So, it's simple arithmetic," he said, pointing to the printers in the middle of the garage. "The juicier the story I write, the more papers I sell. And a guy getting killed over a priceless collection of arrowheads no one even knew existed is pretty juicy. Way better than, like, for example, a love story between the dead guy and the cop investigating his murder."

I looked him in the eye and clenched my teeth to contain the words that came to mind. Something along the lines of *fuck you, you greasy, unibrowed piece of shit.*

"Frau, what the hell are you talking about?"

He lifted an open palm and swiveled in his chair. He took his phone off the desk and tapped it a few times.

"I just sent it to you."

"Sent me what?"

"What I'm talking about."

My phone made its gunshot noise, indicating an incoming message. Frau had sent me a picture and a link to a YouTube video. The photo was dark and pixelated, but I easily recognized Ortega, whispering something in my ear. I opened the link: it was security footage from the Jackaroe, the club where I'd gone dancing the night I'd ended up in Ortega's bed. It was slowed down to play second by second, and you could see me and Julio talking and laughing. *Canoodling*, Aunt Susana would have called it. Every couple of seconds, I'd lean against him to keep my balance. They had been pouring the mojitos a little stronger than usual that night. Ortega whispers something in my ear, and I slowly nod. He walks to the exit. Exactly ninety seconds later, I do the same.

"You uploaded it to YouTube? Are you crazy?" I exclaimed, slamming my phone against the table so hard I was afraid I broke the screen.

"Easy now. It's on private, which means only people I send the link to can see it."

"Where did you get that footage?"

"Aw, Laura. So, there's a thing in journalism called reporter's privilege, which basically means a good journalist respects his sources' privacy. But I can tell you that you can learn a lot from people's social media. Such as, if a guy like Ortega, who usually posts pictures of drinks and casinos, shares a slow song by Roxette and a ballad by Ricardo

Arjona on the same day, you don't have to be a genius to figure something put butterflies in his stomach."

"Yeah, whatever, Jorge, I'm not buying this whole Nancy Drew
routine. Someone told you about that night," I said, thinking about
the Harpy, Isabel Moreno, who had made it clear she knew about my
night with Ortega. Telling a journalist about it only upped the ante in
her favorite game: making my life impossible.

"Like I said, Laura, sources are sacred. And even after I figured
out the date, it's not like it was easy getting the Jackaroe to give me the
footage."

I didn't know what to say. I looked at my phone to see if I'd shattered the screen. I hadn't.

A scratching at the sheet metal garage door interrupted the silence.
Great, he had a dog.

"Camilo!" Frau shouted, and the scratches stopped immediately.
He reclined a little in his chair. "But anyway, all I'm asking for is a little
info."

"You're not asking, you're extorting. I'm a police officer. You do
realize there might be consequences for this, don't you?"

"Hey, Laura, let's take it down a notch, okay? I'm not extorting you.
I talked to a lawyer, and he says no one would call this extortion. I'm
just saying I have to publish something, and I want to let you choose
what it is."

"Not to mention this doesn't prove anything," I continued, ignoring him. "We don't even leave the club together. All that happens is a
guy whispers in my ear. Big deal."

"Maybe not to you, but what about your boss? Would he think it's
a big deal? I don't know a lot about stuff like this, but a police officer
investigating the murder of a guy she slept with two months earlier is a
conflict of interest, isn't it?"

I took a few deep breaths to try to relax. I felt like a total idiot.
How could I have thought my history with Ortega would stay secret

in a town as small as Puerto Deseado? It was a drunk, one-time thing with a guy I didn't give a shit about. If he hadn't shown up murdered two months later, it would have just been an irrelevant, blurry memory.

"Don't look so glum! I promise I'll take the video down today. And obviously I won't name you in anything I write. Anonymous sources all the way. But you have to give me something. Is the arrowhead thing true?"

"How do I know you won't go ahead and publish those images anyway?"

"I give you my word."

"Yeah, that's not worth much to me."

"Just like I protect my sources, I respect my word. Come on, think for a second. It wouldn't be very smart for me to two-time an officer of the law, would it? Definitely not in a town this small."

I looked him in the eyes and spoke slowly, like when I was trying to squeeze a witness so he'd spill. "If any of these images surface today, next month, or ten years from now . . ."

"Laura, you don't have to threaten me. Honest. I'm a man of my word."

I took a few deep breaths, debating between throwing him a bone so he'd let me do my job in peace and busting his head against the table.

"We don't know if they killed him for the arrowheads," I eventually said. "But there's reason to believe Ortega may have been in possession of a case of arrowheads containing several pieces."

"The Panasiuk Collection?"

"We don't know, but it's probable."

"How do the police know there's a collection of arrowheads connected to the crime?"

"Connected to the victim, not to the crime."

"Whatever. How do they know?"

"There was a photo on Ortega's phone," I said, exhaling and showing him the image on my phone. "It's a collection of iridescent arrowheads arranged in a triangle on a red velvet backing."

"That's exactly how they describe the Panasiuk Collection."

There was more scratching at the garage door. Frau closed his eyes, shrugged, and gave me an apologetic look.

"Send me that photo?"

"No way, Jorge. It's evidence in an open case. You can forget about it."

"Fine, I won't pressure you. But I need more to write about."

I had to give him something. Otherwise, I could kiss the investigation goodbye and say hello to a big gaping hole in my career.

"Last night there was a robbery at the museum," I said. "They forced open a window and broke into a glass case. There are thousands of arrowheads there, but the only one they took belongs to the Panasiuk Collection. An archaeologist was working in the building when they broke in. They gagged him, tied him up, and locked him in a cabinet. We found him this morning."

Frau raised his eyebrows and applauded slowly. "Now *that* is juicy. That'll be more than enough for now."

"For now?"

This time the scratching at the door was accompanied by a high-pitched whimper. Frau slapped his knees, muttered under his breath, and walked to the door.

"What do you want, weirdo?" he asked the dog, sliding the door open only a few inches. "Can't you see I'm with someone? Can't you ever behave yourself when—"

Before Frau could finish his sentence, the enormous Saint Bernard pushed its way through the door and ran into the garage. Instinctively, I took refuge behind my chair.

"Don't worry, he's harmless! Camilo, come!"

Camilo let out a deep, resounding bark, took three leaps in my direction, shifted all his weight to his hind legs, and pounced on me. Before I had a chance to react, he landed on my chest, knocking me and the chair to the ground.

"Get him off! Jesus, get him off me!" I shouted as the dog's claws pricked my shoulders and throat.

There was another bark and then a big, slobbery tongue on my face.

"Camilo, what's wrong with you, huh?" Frau yelled, using two hands to pull the dog away by its head. The dog was strong enough to tear Frau's hand off, but it chose to whimper pathetically instead.

Pulling on the collar with all his might, Frau barely managed to get his pet onto the patio. When he came back, he put his hands on his hips and took in the havoc Camilo had wreaked. Each footstep had left a saucer-sized blot of mud on the floor. I got up and saw that the dog had also gotten dirt all over me.

Frau couldn't contain his laughter.

"You think it's funny?"

"Sorry, I'm sorry," he said. "Come on, I'll show you where the bathroom is."

I closed the bathroom door, sat on the counter, and took a deep breath. My legs were trembling, and my reflection in the mirror was pale. I heard Frau reprimanding his dog, which barked and whimpered. The kitchen door closed again, and then there was silence. Frau must have done something to pacify Camilo.

I did the best I could to get the mud off my skin and clothes. I don't know how long I stood there, trying to catch my breath and regain some color in my face. It could have been three minutes or twenty. After a while, I went back to the garage.

Frau didn't look up from his phone when I came in. The chair I'd used to defend myself from Camilo was on the ground, and both the chair and the floor were still covered in mud. As if that weren't enough to remind me of what had just happened, Frau had closed the document on his computer, revealing his desktop wallpaper: a photo of him embracing Camilo.

"Sorry, I just got an important message," he said, putting his phone in his pocket and picking up the chair.

"It's fine, I'm leaving anyway," I said, and I gathered up my things.

CHAPTER 36

Atardecer Ranch was only about twenty miles from Puerto Deseado, but Manuel and I had to travel more than sixty, since to get there by car you had to go west along the north bank of the estuary, cross at the first bridge, then drive all the way back east on gravel roads the whole way. Fortunately, Lamuedra loaned us his personal four-by-four, so we were able to do around forty for most of the drive.

Because of what happened at the museum, we had decided to warn the people at Atardecer Ranch. In fact, we were going to offer to take custody of their iridescent arrowhead to keep it safe.

We spent a few hours trying to call them ahead of our arrival, but we couldn't get through. Echeverría called Castro to ask if there was any other way to reach them, and he said they only got a cell signal from the top of a hill they climbed every morning to check their messages. It was around noon by the time we learned this, which meant they wouldn't get our messages until the following day. We didn't want to risk waiting.

I'd have liked to visit Atardecer Ranch with Castro, who had been doing archaeological work there for years, but he was still in shock, and the doctor had recommended he spend the next forty-eight hours resting. Echeverría and Lamuedra wouldn't let me go alone, so I took Manuel.

After two hours of driving over the gravel, feeling the tires spit stones against the bottom of the truck, we finally saw the roof of the Atardecer Ranch. The only buildings on that thirty-seven-thousand-acre property were a few cement sheds and an out-of-place prefab metal house surrounded by salt cedars. Beside it, several four-by-four trucks were parked beneath bright tarps.

"I'd love to go camping out here. At a different time of year, obviously. I don't know if I love it enough to go in the middle of winter," I said, parking outside the metal house.

"Just say the word and we'll go together. I love camping," responded Manuel.

A man with a brown mustache and a black beret emerged from the house's front door.

"Afternoon, sir," Manuel said, poking his head out the truck window. Something about the scene had prompted him to adopt an exaggerated rural accent.

"Come on out, I don't bite," said the man.

We did as he instructed. He greeted us with a firm handshake and said his name was Herrera.

"You here to camp?"

"No, actually," I said.

There was a flash of disappointment in his brown eyes. "Are you lost?"

"Er, no. We came because we heard you have a small arrowhead museum here."

"We do, but it's only open to campers."

He crossed his arms and looked at his canvas sandals for a few seconds. Then his somber expression turned into a chuckle, which turned into a cough.

"I'm joking. Of course you can see the collection. Though my wife is the real arrowhead fanatic. I don't have anything to do with the things. Come inside," he said, opening the front door of the house.

We stepped into his kitchen, which smelled like they had just been frying something. A woman washing dishes next to a wood-burning stove turned off the water, dried her hands on her apron, and came to greet us.

"This is Lali, my old lady," said Herrera. Then, turning to his wife, he said, "These folks want to see your arrowhead collection."

Manuel and I had decided that before saying anything, we would visit the museum to see how and where they kept the Panasiuk arrowhead. After we knew that, we'd warn them about the risks of keeping it there.

"Wonderful," said Lali. "Are you two arrowhead collectors?"

"I'm not," I said.

"Me neither," said Manuel.

"Well then, get in the truck. We'll start from the beginning."

"We don't have much time," I improvised.

Lali nodded, but there was a trace of confusion on her face, as if she weren't familiar with the concept of not having much time.

"It won't take half an hour, and it'll help you understand what's in the museum," she insisted.

Manuel and I exchanged a look.

"Okay, then," I said. "We'll be driving back after dark anyway."

Lali smiled, gave her husband the briefest possible wave goodbye, and led us out the door.

Lali jumped into Lamuedra's truck and guided us to a well-worn track that went up a small gray hill covered in low shrubs.

At the top of the hill, the landscape changed radically. Along the shoreline, the winter sunshine was hitting the golden sand dunes at a slant. In the distance, hundreds of sea lions luxuriated on a small island.

"Park over here," Lali instructed.

We got out of the truck and followed her down the middle of a sand dune. She walked silently, her gaze fixed on the ground. With almost every step, she crouched to turn over some shred of stone in the sand.

"Most of the pieces you're going to see in our little museum came from right here," she said. "This particular spot is a famous place for finding arrowheads on our property. For thousands of years, this is where the Tehuelche would gather to carve arrowheads."

"And you're still finding pieces after all these years?"

"Oh yes. In fact, every year, archaeologists come all the way from Buenos Aires to do their studies here. I've been coming here for a good forty years now, and I still always find something, because the wind's always pushing these dunes around."

Just then, a far-off groan floated to us on the wind. On the small island in the distance, a sea lion sat up to defend its portion of the rock against another male who was moving in on his turf.

"Look there, a scraper," said Lali, pulling an object out of the sand. "These are much easier to find than arrowheads. They used them to get the last bit of meat off guanaco hide."

Lali handed me the carved rock. Like the countless stones I'd picked up and discarded, it was a grayish green. One end had been struck hundreds of times until it was sculpted to the proper shape, and the other had been cut with one clean blow. Together, the miniscule notches formed a rigid edge that glittered under the sun.

"It's lovely," I said, handing it back to her. She put it in her pocket.

We walked a little farther, at a very slow pace, our eyes fixed on the sand.

"This is an incredible place," I said, looking up. The dunes bordered one of the very few sand beaches within hundreds of miles.

"Tell you the truth, if I'd been a Tehuelche woman, I'd have picked this spot to make my tools, too. There's a gorgeous view, coverage from the wind, and plenty to eat."

As Lali mentioned this last perk, she pointed to the mountains of mussel shells, discolored from years out in the elements.

We walked a bit farther to the last sand dune. Past that, the land turned flat and stuck out in a precipice over the sea. Lali reached into her blue tote bag and took out a thermos, a gourd, and some yerba mate. I made a point of checking the sand around me before sitting down, but I didn't see anything that looked like an arrowhead.

"Shouldn't we get going?" asked Manuel.

"Don't tell me you're going to turn down a nice, warm yerba mate with a view like this!" Lali insisted.

I smiled at her, and the three of us sat facing the ocean. The island with the sea lions was to our right, but the wind had changed course, and we could no longer hear them.

Lali handed me the gourd, which I clutched in both hands to warm my fingers. Then she reached forward and placed her fingers on a small ochre rock less than an inch from my foot. She grinned as she extracted an arrowhead the size of a fingernail from the sand.

"But . . . how did you do that? I looked before I sat down and didn't see anything."

"You must have uncovered it with your feet," said Manuel.

"What are the odds of that?"

"Happens all the time," said Lali between sips of yerba mate. "Once, I even found an arrowhead next to my truck before I got in. The trick is to turn over every single pebble, even if it doesn't look like much. The only thing we arrowhead collectors know for sure is that pieces always turn up where we least expect them."

I looked at the piece my foot had just unearthed. The edge was as delicate as a serrated knife, and it ended in a point that sank into my skin as easy as a pin. Thousands of years ago, someone had carved this work of art in the same place where we were now drinking yerba mate. My heart was beating with an overwhelming feeling of happiness, and I finally understood how searching for arrowheads had become a lifelong passion for Lali, Aunt Susana, and Teodor Panasiuk.

I realized that this kind of discovery was gratifying because it was totally unpredictable. What if we had sat a few feet closer to the sea? I never would have uncovered that piece with my foot, and it might have been another ten years before someone found it. Or another hundred. Or it might have stayed buried forever, captured in the slow migration of the sand dunes.

CHAPTER 37

"Come this way," Lali instructed back at the ranch house.

We parked the truck and walked around the house. Lali turned the knob of a shabby-looking door and pushed it with her shoulder until the hinges finally gave way with a squeak. Inside, a steep stairway led to a square board in the ceiling. Grayish light pierced the cracks.

Lali climbed the stairs and pushed away a beam above her with an open hand.

"Watch your head," she said as she continued up.

We climbed into a small attic so old that the wood floor warped under our feet. A quick glance around was all it took to understand the place's appeal: that stairway was a portal into Patagonia's past.

"So, this is the little museum we've been building up over the years. There's a little bit of everything. There are some old bottles and magazines over there, and this is one of the first record players manufactured in Argentina. There are also pieces from ships that have landed on the beach. I found this bronze porthole last year. And, of course, we have plenty of arrowheads and spears and those sorts of things."

"What would you say is your most special arrowhead?" I asked, trying to get down to business.

Lali went to a shelf full of small metal and wood boxes. She took down an old tuna can, opened it, and showed us three arrowheads on a pad of yellowing cotton.

"That's a hard question to answer. It would be like choosing your favorite child. But there are a few that are very special. These are some of my favorites because they're practically see-through. Some archaeologists have told me they're made with quartz from around here."

Manuel and I took turns examining and praising the pieces. When we gave them back, Lali took down another tuna can that held a black arrowhead barely bigger than the nail of her index finger.

"It's incredible," I said. "I can't wrap my head around how they could make such a perfect point without metal tools or real technology."

"This one's obsidian," said Lali. "Volcanic glass. It's so sharp that until recently they used obsidian scalpels to operate on people's eyes."

"It's so small," said Manuel. "What would they hunt with it?"

"Probably nothing. Once, I was talking to Alberto Castro, an archaeologist who sometimes works around here, and he said little arrowheads like this might have just been ornamental. They'd make them for fun, competing to see who could make the most perfect one."

"Castro was the person who told us about your collection," I said. "I'd heard of it before, but he was the one who suggested we come see you."

"Ah, you know Alberto?"

"Yes. Or, at least, we've known him for a few days."

"Don't tell me he's in Puerto Deseado! That's so odd, he always tells me when he's in town. Every year he comes to check on our collection and look for arrowheads. He almost always brings two or three graduate students and stays for a few days. Whenever they come, I make sure to save the best campsite for them."

"I think it was kind of an impromptu trip. That must be why he didn't mention it."

Lali shrugged. We spent the next fifteen minutes looking at artifacts. Judging by the number of boxes on the shelves, we saw only a small portion of the collection. There were scrapers, arrowheads, and awls of every shape and size. Lali even had what she called recycled pieces, which had been carved for one purpose but then adapted for another.

"You must have a lot of pieces, after forty years," I said after Lali finished explaining the difference between a scraper and an awl.

"So many that I lost count. I have boxes full of them in other parts of the house, but I don't bring them up here because I'm not sure the attic can hold much more weight."

"Would you sell them? I mean, if someone offered to buy one."

"Oh no, that's a big no-no," she said quickly. "It's completely illegal to buy or sell cultural artifacts. And besides, I don't like the thought of them leaving the ranch. Better that they stay here, where I found them."

We spent another quarter hour seeing more arrowheads and other lithic artifacts. Some really were extraordinary, but none matched the ones from the Panasiuk Collection.

"Did you ever find one that had a kind of iridescent color?" I finally asked.

Lali gave me a puzzled look. "You believe in that too?"

"In what?"

"In the legend of Yalen and the iridescent arrowheads."

"Who else believes in it?"

"I don't know, lots of people. Why are you asking me about them?"

It seemed like it was time to tell her why we were really there.

"Lali," I said, "do you have an iridescent arrowhead here or don't you? It's very important. We work for the court, and we're investigating a murder."

Her eyes widened, and she looked at us with a startled expression.

"What are you talking about?" she said, grabbing a rusted cookie tin.

Inside was a small guanaco-hide bag. Lali opened it and let a bluish arrowhead fall into her palm. She lifted it to the window, and the arrowhead transformed the last rays of sun into multicolor sparkles.

That was what we had come for: the ninth arrowhead of the Panasiuk Collection.

"It's amazing," I said, taking it from her hand. "Where did you find it?"

"My father gave it to me in '95."

"Where did he get it?"

"No idea. I tried to get him to tell me, but he just smiled and said, 'Ask no questions and you'll be told no lies.' I guess someone gave it to him, or else he must have bought it. He wasn't as scrupulous as me with that kind of thing."

"And you never asked him again?"

"I didn't have the chance," she explained. "He was very sick when he gave it to me, and he died a few months later."

The three of us were silent for a beat. I twirled the arrowhead between two fingers.

"What was that about a murder?" Lali asked. "I don't see what I would have to do with anything like that."

I quickly explained the case to her, skipping most of the details. I just said that we'd found a body, that a collection of iridescent arrowheads was missing from the victim's house, and that thirteen days later, a similar arrowhead had disappeared from the museum.

"Actually," I said, wrapping up, "that's how Alberto Castro ended up in Puerto Deseado. He's a friend of the judge and came to help as a kind of expert witness."

"Then why didn't he come with you?" she asked, suspicious.

"Because he hasn't been feeling so good since yesterday," I said. I didn't want to alarm her by explaining why. "He told us this is the last piece the attacker would need to complete the Panasiuk Collection. Or, I mean, this one and the one we have at the courthouse as evidence."

"You're scaring me," she said.

"We're not trying to. But since you two are isolated out here in the country, we wanted to warn you as soon as we could. All this happened in the last two weeks. It's possible that whoever committed the murder and robbed the museum is trying to complete the collection. If I were you, I would hide that arrowhead and not show it to anyone for a while. If you want, we can take it with us and keep it somewhere safe until all this is over."

She was shaking her head before I'd even finished my sentence. She closed her hand around the arrowhead and gave us a severe look.

"Thank you for the warning," she said. "The arrowhead will stay here."

"Be very careful, then," I insisted.

"Don't worry. We've lived in the country our whole lives. It wouldn't be the first undesirable we've driven off with a shotgun, and I venture it won't be the last."

CHAPTER 38

The next day, I got to work around seven thirty in the morning. I'd been in the lab for less than five minutes when my phone rang.

"Hello?" I answered, surprised to be called so early.

"Laura, can you come to my chambers for a moment?"

"Sure, I'm coming now."

I'm fucked, I thought when I hung up. I'd promised Echeverría that when I got back from Calafate, I'd give her the fingerprints from Ortega's house, the ones that had magically disappeared from the evidence folder.

I took the stairs slowly, trying to think of a new excuse. It didn't make sense to look for them again or to think about where I might have lost them. I'd already turned over half the courthouse.

I opened the door to Echeverría's chambers with no idea what I was going to say. She was in her desk chair. Across from her was Lamuedra, who was crossing his arms. When I came in, he looked me up and down before exhaling impatiently through his nose.

"Laura, sit down," Echeverría said, indicating the empty chair next to Lamuedra. "You know why I want to speak with you, I assume?"

I nodded.

"And?"

"I looked for them everywhere, Your Honor, I swear, but I can't find them. I don't know what could have happened. All I did was lift them from the broken glass, transfer them to a piece of card stock, and put them in the evidence folder. Then, when Manuel went to get photographs so we could digitize them, they were gone."

"Wait, you mean you also lost the only forensic evidence we have in the Ortega case?"

"Wasn't that why you called me?"

The three of us were silent. Lamuedra squeezed the bridge of his nose between his index finger and thumb.

"I didn't lose them," I added. "They disappeared. I can't explain it, but they can't be lost."

"Christ!" exclaimed Echeverría. "Maybe you should try being careful every once in a while. You can't just fuck up this badly twice in a row."

"Twice in a row? What are you talking about? I thought this was why you called me here."

"No, Badía, we called you here so you could tell us where the hell the editor of *El Orden* got this photo," said Lamuedra.

Echeverría turned her computer monitor around so I could see it. I recognized the amateurish appearance of the newspaper's website. A photo of the Panasiuk Collection took up half the screen. The headline— all caps, blue against a gray background—was a question.

WAS THERE A MURDER IN OUR CITY OVER A MYTHICAL
ARROW COLLECTION?

"I hadn't seen this" was all I could say.

"Well, have at it," Lamuedra said. Echeverría tossed me the mouse.

I read the article in silence, listening to my two bosses breathing. It felt like a noose was tightening around my neck.

Saturday morning, our publication received a photo-graph related to the investigation of the homicide of Julio Ortega, a local store owner who was found lifeless in his house on Estrada Street on August 7. According to people close to the victim, he was found beaten to death. The local police have not yet revealed their motive for the crime.

The above photograph (which will also be printed next Saturday in our print edition) was found on the victim's phone and could be considered the first possible explanation of Ortega's brutal murder. It shows the mystical Panasiuk Collection, a collection of opal arrowheads which were thought, until today, to exist only in pencil sketches. In addition to their historical value (see the sidebar "A Cursed Collection"), local lithic art collectors have informed us that the arrowheads could be sold for as much as ten million US dollars if sold illegally on the black market.

Furthermore, our town's own local Mario Brozoski Museum was recently robbed, as part of a series of events which appear highly likely to be related to the case. Early Saturday morning, archaeologist Alberto Castro, the world's most respected expert in the world of lithic Tehuelche art, was working in the museum when it was allegedly broken into by a masked man who gagged Castro, tying him up and locking him in a cabinet after forcing his way in through a window. Only one of the institution's almost ten thousand pieces was stolen. Given the characteristics of the stolen arrowhead, which was shaped like a leaf and carved in iridescent stone, it is believed to belong to the infamous Panasiuk Collection.

As for official sources, Police Commissioner Lamuedra had no comment as to whether the arrowheads are considered a motive for the murder of local Puerto Deseado resident Julio Ortega by the police.

"Want to explain what the fuck this is, Badía?" asked Lamuedra.

To buy myself time, I read the sidebar, "A Cursed Collection," which was a mishmash of all the urban legends surrounding the collection. It gave a colorful account of Yalen's murder by his brother, Magal, and told how Teodor Panasiuk was so obsessed with completing the collection that he traded a house for a single arrowhead.

I went back to the first article and looked at the photo of the collection. It was absolutely the one we had found on Ortega's phone. I knew exactly what had happened, though deep down I refused to admit it. I didn't want to acknowledge, even to myself, that I had been so stupid.

Two days earlier, I'd shown that photo to Jorge Frau. He had asked me for a copy and I had refused. Then his Saint Bernard knocked me onto the floor, and I remembered noticing that, when I got back from the bathroom, there was no longer an open document on Frau's monitor. While I was cleaning up and regaining my composure, that piece of shit had connected my phone to his computer with a USB cord and copied the picture.

"We don't know who Ortega sent that photo to before he was killed," I offered.

"The article says the image was found on the victim's phone. How could the paper have found that out? And, even more inexplicably, it gives a play-by-play of Castro getting tied up in the museum. Practically no one knows about that," said Echeverría.

"I don't know what could have happened."

"Well, you better find out. This is your responsibility, Laura. The only people who had access to that photo were Manuel, you, and me. It wasn't me. And if Manuel is the screwup, that's still on you."

I was about to add that her archaeologist buddy Castro also had access to the photo, but then I remembered that his was watermarked. The photo in *El Orden* wasn't. It had come from my phone.

Lamuedra joined in: "Laura, if you fuck up half this bad again, you're off the case and I'm making you eat two weeks' suspension. Amateur hour is over. Got it?"

"Yes, Commissioner."

All I could do was contain the lump in my throat until I got out of the judge's chambers. By the time I closed the door behind me, tears were about to roll down my cheeks.

"Day off to a bad start?" the Harpy asked. She had just arrived and was settling in at her desk.

I walked quickly to my lab, shut the door, and gave a short sob, just enough to get it out. I was ashamed for having let Frau steal that photo off my phone and for not being able to find the fingerprints that were essential to solving the case.

I decided to search the lab one last time. I looked under all the equipment and in every folder. I even emptied the cabinet where I had put the fingerprints and tilted it over to check underneath. After searching for an hour, I concluded, once again, that they weren't there. And if Manuel was telling the truth when he said he never took them out of the cabinet, then someone else must have. But who? And why?

It wasn't long before I remembered Isabel Moreno's threat. "This isn't over" is what she'd said after our fight. I could imagine her spitefully telling Frau about me and Ortega, but I never thought she'd stoop to stealing key evidence just to hurt me.

I came up with a plan. I scanned the objects on my desk, trying to decide which would be most useful as a tool in my plan to expose her. I chose the coffee mug.

CHAPTER 39

I polished the outside of the mug until I could almost see my reflection in it. Then I pressed my index finger against it over and over again, until it looked like it belonged to a greasy-handed two-year-old. I opened my fingerprint kit and brushed the entire surface with black dust. Now it looked like it belonged to a mechanic.

I lifted several of the fingerprints with tape and transferred them to a piece of card stock identical to the one that had gone missing. Above the prints I clearly wrote "JULIO ORTEGA HOMICIDE." By the time I'd cleaned the mug and put the kit back in its aluminum case, it was almost ten. Perfect timing.

A few minutes later, Manuel stuck his head into the lab, like he did every day at ten.

"Stop the presses, it's coffee time!"

His eyes landed on the fingerprints, which I'd left on the table.

"Wait," he said, coming in and picking them up, "these aren't the ones you lost, are they?"

"No, those are gone forever. But it turns out that I'd only lifted prints off one side of two of the shards," I said, pointing to the reconstructed pane that was still on the table. "And we're in luck, because there were a lot of prints."

"I should photograph them, right?"

"Right, but first you should make me some coffee."

"Happy to."

"Go get it started. I have to send an email and then I'll join you in the kitchen."

Once he was gone, I looked around and decided to use the fern Aunt Susana had given me. It was showing signs of neglect, but it was still generally leafy. I opened a box and took out the camera Manuel and I used to photograph victims and evidence. Incidentally, it also took excellent videos. I made sure there was enough memory left on the card and put it into motion-sensor mode so that it would only begin filming once someone entered its field of view. I hid it among the fern's green leaves, with the lens pointing at the cabinet that the first set of fingerprints had disappeared from.

I put my decoy fingerprints on the middle shelf, closed the cabinet, and left the keys in the lock. Then I went to the kitchen.

CHAPTER 40

Manuel was saying something to Isabel Moreno, and both of them were giggling. As soon as he saw me come in, his demeanor chilled noticeably. He knew that the Harpy and I could barely stand the sight of each other, and he was clearly debating between getting her into bed and keeping me as a friend.

The scene was about to get awkward, but fortunately some other court employees showed up, and soon all ten of the chairs around the large table were occupied. Most of us were drinking coffee, though there was also a group of three yerba mate diehards. Even the police who guarded the courthouse door usually joined the daily ritual for a few minutes.

"Oh, Laura, it sure is a shame that the paper somehow got a hold of that photo, isn't it?" said Isabel in front of everyone, hiding a smile behind her coffee mug.

"Yeah, how do you figure they got it?" asked Ramiro Carabajal, one of the court's five administrative employees. His job essentially consisted of preparing Word documents, but he also had a master's degree in collecting and redistributing gossip. Having him and the Harpy for an audience suited my purposes beautifully.

"I have no idea, honestly," I said.

"Is it true that you also lost some evidence?" asked Isabel.

I looked her in the eyes, but I couldn't tell if her gleeful expression came from ridiculing me in front of everyone or from knowing that she herself had made the prints disappear.

"It is. I had some fingerprints from the crime scene and now I can't find them anywhere. It's like they vanished into thin air. Fortunately, I found some more prints on a piece of glass I forgot to analyze."

"Seems like Little Miss Investigator has been a little distracted at work. Head in the clouds?" she said sarcastically.

I ignored her and described how I had "forgotten" to lift these new fingerprints, the same story I'd told Manuel a few minutes earlier.

"And I'm sure you took photos right away this time, right?" the Harpy asked.

"Not yet. I'm going to do it as soon as I find the camera, which has also disappeared."

There was a murmur around the table.

"You're not afraid lightning might strike twice?"

"No, Isabel, I'm sure as hell not losing them again. In fact, I want all of you to be my witnesses, just in case: I put them in the same cabinet in my lab where I had put the others."

I made a show of checking the time on my phone and lifting my eyebrows.

"Shoot, I have to go. Manuel, I don't think I'll be back today. I have a lot of work to do in town. I'll see you tomorrow. Bye, everybody."

I left the kitchen, leaving behind half a cup of coffee. I went by the lab to grab my things and noticed that my desk drawer was half-open. I looked inside, panicking. Someone had taken the plastic box with the arrowhead we'd found at the scene of the crime.

I locked the door and took the camera out from behind the fern. I turned on my computer, ignored four new emails, and inserted the memory card. The camera had recorded a thirty-second video.

I clearly wasn't crazy. Someone had come in and taken the arrowhead while I was in the kitchen. Even though I'd pointed the camera at the cabinet and not my desk, I easily recognized the figure who came into the lab and opened the drawer. It was Delia Echeverría.

I ran up the stairs to her chambers and went in without knocking. She was reading a document, with her glasses resting on the tip of her nose.

"Laura, what do you need?" she said with a disconcerting smile.

"The arrowhead" was all I could say.

Continuing to smile, she gave me a thumbs-up. "Good, good. That makes me very happy. I was afraid you wouldn't notice it was missing, or that you'd hide it from me if you did."

"You mean it was you?"

"Yes. I mean, no. I mean, I didn't have anything to do with the fingerprints, obviously. But I did take the arrowhead."

"To see if I'd tell you it was missing?"

She laughed. "No, that was just a bonus. I took it to keep it safe."

"From what?"

"Well, assuming that the person who took Julio Ortega's arrowheads was also the person who robbed the museum, they only need two more pieces to complete the collection."

"The one at the Atardecer Ranch and the one you just took from the lab," I said.

"Exactly. I know we have police security here twenty-four hours a day, but I still think it's wise to keep the evidence someplace a little safer than your desk drawer." She pointed to the large iron safe in the corner of the room. "Let me know whenever you need it and I'll get it for you. But let's only do that when it's strictly necessary. We know that it's a key piece in a very valuable puzzle, and if we lose it, lots of heads are going to roll, including mine."

I told her that was an excellent idea. In the past, before the fingerprints had vanished, she never would have taken that kind of liberty without talking to me first. But it seemed better not to mention that.

I went back to the lab, put the camera back behind the fern, and turned it on.

CHAPTER 41

Between the stench emanating from Enrique Vera's immense, filthy body and the odor of recently applied disinfectant, the air in the interrogation room was foul.

The police had found Vera hiding at an abandoned construction site on the outskirts of town. A neighbor reported seeing someone lighting a fire there three nights in a row. We knew Vera couldn't have gotten very far, because he wouldn't have had time to grab his wallet or anything else on the morning we'd gone looking for him at his house. We'd guessed that if he was guilty, he would hide out until things cooled down, then sneak back into his house for his things. But we never thought he'd wait it out in such precarious conditions.

When they brought him to the station, we spent a few minutes removing the grimy rag he had used to bandage a deep wound in his calf. He said he'd cut it falling off the embankment behind his house three days earlier.

"You're legally entitled to be taken to a hospital," said Lamuedra.

Vera shook his head. One of his hands was chained to the loop in the middle of the stainless steel table. He used the other to throw the improvised, browned bandage into a small wastebasket by his chair. I soaked a new one in disinfectant and gave it to him. When he placed it on the wound, he couldn't quite contain a grunt of pain.

"Let's begin then," said Lamuedra. "I'm going to ask you a simple question, and I want you to think long and hard before you answer me. What you say will be recorded and sent straight to the court. Judges don't like liars. If you don't believe me, ask Detective Badía. She works with one."

I said nothing. Lamuedra swept the room with his eyes before speaking. He was making sure the red light on the camera hanging from the ceiling was turned off, but Vera didn't seem to notice. Interrogating a suspect without his lawyer present was, at best, unorthodox.

"Where were you before dawn on August seventh?"

Silence.

"Actually, we might as well skip the theatrics. Did you beat Julio Ortega to death?"

Before speaking, Vera rubbed his dirt-strewn, greasy forehead with his free hand.

"No."

"What blood type are you? In case you need a transfusion," I asked, pointing to his injury.

"A-negative."

"Huh," I said. "As I'm sure you can imagine, there was blood all over Ortega's clothes, on the floor, and on the sofa. Buckets of O-positive. But we also found a drop of someone else's blood. Want to guess what type it was?"

"I'm the only A-negative in Puerto Deseado?"

We know it's your blood, I thought, but I couldn't say it. The DNA tests I'd ordered were totally illegal, and admitting that to Vera could compromise the entire case.

"If you didn't do it, why'd you run away when we came to your house?"

He was silent.

"How's your ear healing?" I asked, pointing to his right earlobe, which was no longer bandaged as it had been in the casino. I could clearly see an ochre scar down the middle, like someone had ripped out a piercing. That was probably where the drop of blood in Ortega's house had come from.

"Look, we know Ortega owed you lots of money," said Lamuedra.

"Doesn't mean I killed him."

"He had marks on his hands," I said. "They were a week or two old. Like someone had taken a drill to his palms to torture him."

"I don't know what you're talking about."

"You know that denying everything won't be enough to get you off, right?"

"Someone see me beating the fucker up? Or drilling his hands? You have any kind of actual proof?"

All three of us were silent for a few seconds. Vera was guilty and we knew it, but it wouldn't matter if we couldn't get him to confess.

"It's your blood," I said finally. "Remember that day I saw you at the casino? Your Coke can ended up in my lab. The DNA in your saliva matches the blood we found at Ortega's house."

Lamuedra looked at his feet and breathed through his nose. I could tell he was repressing the urge to throttle me. What I'd just said could complicate the trial, but we didn't have any other choice. If we didn't squeeze him hard enough to get something concrete, he'd never say anything and we wouldn't be able to convince Echeverría to order another, admissible DNA test through the proper channels.

Clearly, Lamuedra didn't share this perspective. He didn't even turn to look at me, and I figured he was reserving his fury for when we were alone.

"Okay, we had a fight. But I didn't kill him," Vera said after a while.

"Can you elaborate on that a little? Why'd you go to his house that night?"

"He called me over. He owed me money, yeah. A lot. Almost forty thousand dollars. I'd been giving him ultimatums for weeks."

"Ultimatums involving a drill?"

"I went because he asked me to come," Vera continued, ignoring me. "He was pretty drunk. A little geeked up, too, I think."

"Geeked up?" asked Lamuedra.

"On cocaine," said Vera. "I could be wrong, though."

I remembered that both substances had appeared in Luis's toxicology report.

"He took me to the dining room and sat next to some papers on his couch. I asked if he had the money. He said he didn't. He said he never would."

"How did you react?"

"I told him I was going to sue. I had promissory notes he signed. But he laughed and gave me the papers on the sofa."

Vera was frowning, and his gaze was distant, the way people look when they're trying to focus on a blurry memory.

"It was bank statements and a letter from the AFIP saying to pay taxes his store owed. He told me he didn't have shit and said the house was in his great-aunt's name. Then he laughed and threw an eight ball at my feet . . . cocaine," he clarified, looking at Lamuedra. "He said that it, his furniture, and a little bit of inventory at Impekable was all that was left for me. He said to take it and leave him alone."

He leaned his forehead against his fists and exhaled loudly. His broad back deflated. I decided to strike while he was vulnerable.

"What did you feel when he said that?"

"Stuck. And angry. Fucking angry."

He was choking up. He lifted his head for a second, his eyes glassy. Seeing someone so brawny on the verge of tears was disconcerting, as if muscles and crying were somehow incompatible. He put his head back down and said nothing for a long time. Only two parts of his body were moving: his shoulders, as he breathed, and his square jaw, which trembled uncontrollably.

"Fucking competition . . . ," he babbled.

"What's that?" asked Lamuedra, but I quickly gestured at him to keep quiet.

The first sob finally came after another minute of silence. It wasn't exaggerated; it was just a groan and a couple of tears. The kind of crying men do when they're ashamed of crying.

"If I hadn't signed up for that fucking competition . . ."

"What're you talking about, Enrique?" I asked.

"I was training for Mr. Patagonia. A bodybuilding competition. It's in Caleta Olivia this year. I had four months to prep and I'd just started a cycle of some new steroids that are supposed to be real good for bulking up without retaining liquid. You need that shit now."

"Illegal steroids, I'm guessing?"

"They're legal. For veterinary use."

"You were on horse drugs?"

"Yeah, and some other shit."

"What other shit?"

"After I finished this year's first steroid program, I started a hormonal regulator regimen. And I was injecting insulin and HGH. None of this would have happened if it wasn't for the HGH."

"Human growth hormone?"

"Yeah. It's the best for if you want to get big. It and steroids are basically required if you want to compete regionally or higher. But it's fucking expensive."

"How expensive?"

"Seven thousand dollars a month."

Lamuedra and I exchanged a look.

"Messi wouldn't play for Barcelona if it wasn't so expensive. Nobody wanted to sign him when they found out he had growth problems. No Argentinian team would pay for the treatment. So his parents didn't think twice when Barcelona offered to."

"Vera, why are you talking about Messi?" said Lamuedra, losing patience.

"So you understand. If I didn't get what Ortega owed me, I couldn't buy the two months of HGH I needed to finish the regimen. And if I didn't finish the regimen, I would've been screwed at the competition."

"You mean you busted open a guy's head to win a beefcake competition in Caleta Olivia?"

Vera shook his head. "You . . . you don't understand."

"No shit I don't understand!" shouted Lamuedra, clapping his hands together violently. "How the fuck are we supposed—"

"HGH is just part of it. It's also the steroids. They get you big fast, and they're not as expensive. But there's lots of side effects. I had just started a cycle with a brand I'd never used before. It made my head burn. I don't know how to explain it to someone not in that world. When you take them, you almost don't recognize yourself. I was pissy all the time. I would've fucked a guy up for bumping into me on the street."

"I don't know how much good that'll do you with the judge," said Lamuedra.

I couldn't tell if Lamuedra was wrong or just bluffing. When I was getting my degree, we looked at lots of cases where being under the influence of steroids was considered a mitigating circumstance.

"So, you got pissed off and beat him to death."

Vera was looking at the chain that held him to the table, but his focus was someplace else, far from the interrogation room.

"Did you kill him or didn't you?" persisted Lamuedra. "Before, you said you didn't, but you can still tell us the truth. The best thing you can do for yourself right now is set the record straight. The more you lie, the harder it's going to be for you later. It's not me and Detective Badía you should be worrying about, it's the trial."

Vera twirled one of the links of his chain between his fingers, like he was trying to tune a radio. The movement got faster and faster, and the chain started to rattle. Then he stopped, sighed heavily, and spoke without looking up.

"I didn't realize it was as much as it was. Like, I just wanted to put a scare in him, so he'd think of some way of getting me my money. I didn't mean to go so far. It was like I lost sense of time for a few minutes. And then it . . . it was too late."

"So, you killed him."

"Yeah, but . . . you have to believe me. I didn't want to do that to him. I'm not a monster."

Vera's face suddenly froze in a familiar expression. It was a face I'd seen on lots of suspects when they realized they'd said too much.

"I need to make a phone call," he said. "I need to talk to Sergio Bugarti, my lawyer."

"Of course," conceded Lamuedra, standing up. "I'll get you a phone. But first, one more question. What did you do with the arrowheads?"

"What arrowheads?"

Lamuedra ran his hands over his head and through his hair, making an exasperated sound. "Vera, I'm trying not to let the fact that you thrashed a person for money interfere with my professionalism. But it's nearly one in the morning and I don't feel like getting my balls busted. I'm going to pretend I didn't hear you and ask again. What did you do with the arrowheads?"

"I don't know . . . I don't know what you're talking about. I swear," answered Vera. If the bewildered look on his face wasn't genuine, he deserved an Academy Award.

"The Panasiuk Collection!" roared Lamuedra, slamming a fist on the table. "The collection of opal arrowheads that disappeared from Ortega's house the night you killed him."

"The thing on the floor?"

I pulled up the article in *El Orden* on my phone and let him read it.

"Yeah, that's it," he said. "I remember it was on the floor, leaning against the wall. I didn't take it. Why would I want that?"

"Because a single one of those arrowheads is worth more than what Ortega owed you."

Vera's pupils grew wide, but he didn't say anything. His lips very slowly curved into a strange grimace and eventually into a smile. He shook his head.

"If I had known he had something worth that much, why would I have beat him up? I could just take it and leave."

The three of us fell silent. What Vera said made sense; something told me that he wasn't lying, that we'd found the killer but not the thief.

"Was there glass?" I asked. "Were the arrowheads behind a pane of glass?"

"Yeah. I think so. What does that have to do with anything? I want to talk to my lawyer. I'm not saying another word until he's here."

Lamuedra and I looked at each other. If Vera was telling the truth and the collection was undisturbed when he left the house, that meant someone went in afterward and took it. Though that still didn't explain why the glass was broken and swept up.

We left Vera. Through the little window into the interrogation room, we saw that he was still shaking his head, no doubt imagining how things would have gone that night if only he'd known what we just told him.

◆ ◆ ◆

After I filled out the paperwork to keep Enrique Vera in detention, Lamuedra called me into his office.

"Congratulations, Laura," he said with a barely discernible smile. I sat on the other side of his desk. "You did an excellent job."

"Thank you. But we still don't know what happened to the arrowheads."

Lamuedra lifted a hand to shut me up. "And that's a question for you to tackle tomorrow. But right now, I'd like you to take five minutes and celebrate the fact that you just solved the most important piece of the puzzle."

"If we find the arrowheads, we'll find whoever attacked Castro—"

Lamuedra raised both of his hands, and also his voice. "Tomorrow, Laura. That's for tomorrow. You just solved one of the most brutal murders in Puerto Deseado's history. It's time to pull your head out of the case and breathe for a minute before plunging back in. I want you to go home and rest."

I told him I would, but both of us knew perfectly well that I wouldn't get a minute of sleep that night.

CHAPTER 42

I got to the courthouse early Tuesday morning. After closing the door to my lab, I fell into my swivel chair with a groan. My legs had been killing me since the day I'd chased Vera through the gorge. The sleepless night certainly hadn't helped, but at least I'd spent it thinking about where I wanted to take the investigation next.

We had found Ortega's killer, so that part of the case was closed. But we still didn't know what had become of the arrowheads. We also technically didn't know whether the person who stole the arrowheads was the same person who had attacked Castro and robbed the museum, but anything else seemed too far-fetched.

I decided to start by looking at photos of the crime scene. Maybe I'd missed something, or maybe some prior detail would prove more meaningful in light of what we had learned.

The obsolete hunk of hardware where the photos were saved was taking too long to boot, so I went to get the printed copies from the evidence folder.

I opened the cabinet and froze. The fake fingerprints were gone. I took two steps to the fern, felt around in its leaves, and removed the hidden camera, which I promptly dropped. My hands were shaking. On my second attempt, I managed to open the side compartment and push the memory card in with my fingernail. The small piece of plastic, which held the answers to all my questions, was ejected with a click.

The three minutes my computer took to finish booting lasted an eternity. When I was finally able to open the contents of the card, I saw that it held three separate files. The camera was configured to start recording whenever it detected motion and to stop recording after five minutes of stillness. It saved each of these sessions as a different file. I double-clicked the newest file and saw myself entering the lab, just a few minutes earlier.

I deleted the file and played the next. In the corner of the screen, the time stamp showed that it was a quarter past five in the afternoon. Mirna, the cleaning lady, came in and vacuumed the lab. She was there for four minutes and never so much as looked at the cabinet, nor did she touch anything on the tables or desks (as she had received strict instructions not to). Five minutes after she vacuumed, the recording ended.

I opened the last file. The time stamp read 2:17 a.m. The silhouette of a male figure entered the lab and turned on the light, his back to the camera. I recognized the blue uniform and black boots. It was one of the policemen on guard duty that night. There was something familiar about his round body and thinning, short hair, but I couldn't tell who it was.

He walked right up to the cabinet, opened it, and rummaged around for a few seconds until he found the card with the fingerprints. He examined it for a few seconds, folded it in four, and put it in his pants pocket. Then he turned around, and I saw his face for a few precious seconds. Long enough to recognize him.

The person who had just taken the bait was none other than Sergeant Debarnot. The person who had found Julio Ortega's body fifteen days earlier.

CHAPTER 43

Lamuedra checked his phone again. It was almost eight o'clock at night. Debarnot would show up for work in the next ten minutes.

When I told him what had happened, Lamuedra personally went looking for Debarnot at his house, but Debarnot's wife said he had taken one of their daughters to the park. After confirming that she was telling the truth, Lamuedra decided to change strategies and wait for Debarnot to come in for his shift at the station. That way he avoided creating a family scandal and minimized the chances of some pseudo-journalist or nosy neighbor finding out that the cops were arresting one of their own.

"Play it again," he said, leaning against the polished wood surface of his desk at the station.

"It's him. It's absolutely, positively him, Commissioner."

"I said show it to me again."

I took the laptop out of my bag, put it on the desk, and played the recording for the hundredth time. We silently watched the forty-five-second video in which Debarnot clearly stole the fake evidence.

"What a fucking disgrace," Lamuedra snarled. "On top of defaming the Santa Cruz Police Force, which has provided for him since he was child, he's disgraced his dead father. I swear, if Flaco Debarnot could, he'd rise from the tomb and kick that ingrate's ass from here to Rio de Janeiro."

Lamuedra's phone rang. He pressed it to his ear.

"I'm coming," he said, already standing up. He turned to me. "Debarnot is in the interrogation room."

CHAPTER 44

The interrogation room hadn't changed much in the twenty hours since we'd had Vera in there, though now there were two cops guarding the door instead of one. The taller of the two was holding a piece of ice wrapped in a paper towel to his forehead.

"Don't tell me he hit you," said Lamuedra.

"He was a little surprised to be grabbed as he entered the station, sir."

"We had to cuff him," said the other officer, putting his own wrists together to demonstrate.

I looked through the interrogation room window. Debarnot's uniform was wrinkled from the struggle with his fellow police officers.

"Don't worry, Ramírez," said Lamuedra, pointing to the injury on the tall cop's forehead. "I'll add it to his tab."

He opened the door and gestured for me to follow him.

"What's going on, Commissioner?" asked Debarnot.

"The questions come from *this* side of the table," Lamuedra said, pointing down at his perfectly polished shoes and giving Debarnot an icy look. "The answers come from your side."

Lamuedra turned toward me, expecting me to say something, but all I did was place my laptop on the table. Debarnot looked on in silence, his eyes shifting between me and Lamuedra every few seconds.

"Recognize this guy?" Lamuedra said, pressing play.

Debarnot watched the video of his own silhouette approaching the cabinet. Before we even got to the part where we saw his face, he leaned forward, put his elbows on the table, and held his face in his shackled hands. The only sound in the room was the jingling of the chain that tethered him to the metal hoop on the table.

"Who're you protecting, Debarnot? Whose fingerprints did you steal?" demanded Lamuedra.

Debarnot sunk his head deeper in his hands and breathed deep. "I don't know what I was thinking, Commissioner."

"I asked you a question, Debarnot. Whose fingerprints are they?" Lamuedra insisted.

Debarnot lifted his glassy brown eyes until his gaze met Lamuedra's. "They're mine," he said, maintaining eye contact.

"*You* were involved in the death of Julio Ortega?" brayed Lamuedra, so loud that the last few syllables came out in falsetto. "You, a police officer?"

Debarnot quickly shook his head and lifted his cuffed hands, showing us his palms. "No, no, I wasn't, Commissioner, I didn't kill him, I swear. He was already dead when I got there. It was like I told you, I was passing by and I thought it was suspicious that the door was open in the middle of winter, so I went in and found Ortega's body. I swear on my daughters, Commissioner, I never touched him, I swear."

Lamuedra crossed his arms.

"The first thing I did was call the station and tell them to send someone. And then while I was waiting, I saw the case with the arrowheads. It was on the floor, in a corner of the dining room. I made a mistake, I know that I shouldn't have even touched it, but it was like an impulse I couldn't control."

"An impulse?"

"I feel so ashamed to be telling you this."

"If I were you I'd feel sick to my stomach," said Lamuedra. "But we're not here to listen to you talk about your feelings. Tell us what you did."

"Marina's dad . . . ," Debarnot muttered, almost inaudibly. "Marina's dad collects arrowheads."

"You stole the collection to score points with your father-in-law?" I asked, emphasizing the word *stole*.

He closed his eyes for a second. He looked like someone who was genuinely sorry for what he'd done but knew it was too late.

"Yes. There's no other word for what I did. I picked up the collection and took it to my car. I was so nervous that I accidentally hit it against a wall as I was leaving, and the glass broke. I searched for a broom to clean it up," he said, anticipating my next question, "but I'd barely started sweeping when I heard the siren."

Lamuedra looked at me. "That explains the broken glass and the broom."

"What did you do with the fingerprints you stole from my cabinet?" I asked.

Debarnot looked at his hands for a second and closed his eyes before speaking. "I burned them. I was afraid that when you found my prints on the glass, you'd think I had something to do with the murder."

"And you claim you didn't?" asked Lamuedra.

"I swear I didn't. It's like I told you, he was dead when I found him. Taking the arrowheads was a stupid mistake. I don't know how to begin to ask for forgiveness. But you have to believe me, Commissioner, from one police officer to another, you have to know that I would never do something like that."

"In my book, a thief is the exact opposite of a police officer," said Lamuedra. "And you're worse than a thief, you're a repeat offender."

"Repeat offender? What do you mean?"

"You assaulted a man, Sergeant! You unlawfully detained the archaeologist Alberto Castro at the museum. You stuck him in a cabinet and tied his hands and feet so you could steal a cultural artifact. What excuse do you have for that? You liked the collection so much you couldn't resist the temptation to complete it? Was some irresistible force seducing you into gathering them all in one place, like this is *The Lord of the* fucking *Rings?*"

"No, Commissioner. I had nothing to do with the museum."

Lamuedra clasped his hands together and rested his chin on them. He exhaled loudly through his nose. "Listen, Debarnot, I'm going to make myself very clear. I don't know what irks me more, what you did or the fact that now you're treating us like idiots. Obviously you won't wear a badge again for the rest of your miserable life, but I want worse for you. You personally deceived me. You betrayed the police force and all of your fellow officers. And if that wasn't enough, you insulted the memory of your old man. I can't wrap my head around the fact that an unparalleled officer like him could have produced something as pitiful as you."

"You're right, Commissioner, this mistake should cost me more than just my job, and I take full responsibility. But I'm not a killer. And I didn't rob the museum."

"Let's say you're telling the truth," I interjected. "Then where are the arrowheads you stole?"

"I don't know. I sold them a few days after I found them."

"You didn't *find* them, Mariano, you *stole* them," corrected Lamuedra. "And I thought you said you took them to impress your father-in-law."

"I got scared and wanted to get rid of them as fast as possible. I regretted everything I did, but by then it was too late."

"Who did you sell them to?"

"I don't know. I put an ad on Mercado Fácil, and a few hours later a guy sent me a message offering me good money for them if I'd take down the ad. I accepted."

That perfectly matched Menéndez-Azcuénaga's story: an online ad for the arrowheads that was taken down in less than a day.

"But you must have seen the buyer's face when you gave them to him," I said.

Debarnot shook his head. "He said to meet him on Route 3, a few miles before Caleta Olivia, under the willow trees."

We all knew exactly what willow trees Debarnot was referring to. In one of the most arid inhabited locations on Earth, those willow trees were the only geographic feature on an eight-hundred-mile stretch of asphalt.

"I didn't see his face. He was wearing a ski mask, and he barely talked. He asked for the arrowheads, looked at them for a long time, then gave me the money and gestured for me to leave."

"How much did he pay you?" I asked, out of curiosity more than anything else.

Debarnot fidgeted in his chair, uncomfortable. "A lot."

"How much."

"Fifty thousand."

"Dollars?"

"No, pesos."

I did the math in my head. That wasn't even three thousand dollars. Less than a hundredth of what Ariel said the collection was worth. Clearly, Debarnot had no idea what he was selling.

"What can you tell us about him? Eye color? Voice?"

"Brown eyes. Man's voice. I don't know anything else. He barely talked to me."

"Body type?"

"Medium build. Five foot eight, maybe."

"Would you say he was really buff? Like he spent a lot of time at the gym?" I wanted to know.

"No, I didn't notice any muscles. He seemed like he was in good shape, though."

"Approximate age?"

"I have no idea. I didn't even see his teeth. He was wearing the kind of ski mask that doesn't have a mouth hole. He was obviously afraid of being recognized."

"Or maybe he was afraid of being seen engaging in black market dealings with an officer of the law!" bellowed Lamuedra.

"He wouldn't have had any way of knowing I was a police officer."

"Which way did he drive after buying the arrowheads?" I asked.

"I don't know. He made me leave first."

"What kind of car was he driving?"

"He didn't have one."

"What do you mean, he didn't have one?" I asked, incredulous. "You met him in the middle of nowhere."

"We did the transaction under the bridge, and there wasn't a car there or on the side of the road. There's no way to hide a car around there, especially not in the middle of the day."

Debarnot was right. Route 3 goes through featureless mesa; there was no way to hide something as big as a car. The bridge he was talking about goes over a river that has dried up completely, except when it rains.

"Someone must have driven him there and then picked him up. So I wouldn't recognize his car, I think," said Debarnot. "He was so careful about not being identifiable, I think he must be from town."

"Assuming you're telling the truth—"

"I'm telling the truth," he interrupted.

"Assuming you're telling the truth," I continued, "the person who bought the arrowheads would have been in Puerto Deseado three days ago. It has to be the same person who stole the other piece from the museum. What color was the ski mask?"

"Gray, I think."

"All gray?"

Debarnot looked at the ceiling, trying to conjure up the image. His eyes moved erratically, with the desperation of a man trying to reverse the irreversible damage he'd done.

"Yes. There was a black lining around the eyes. The rest was gray."

Lamuedra and I exchanged a look. That was exactly how Castro had described the ski mask of the man who had locked him in a cabinet three days earlier.

CHAPTER 45

Before we finished speaking with Debarnot, Lamuedra informed him that, effective immediately, he was relieved of his duties indefinitely. There would be criminal proceedings for robbery and for obstruction of justice, in addition to, and exacerbated by, abuse of his authority as a member of the police force. Debarnot acknowledged that he understood, and Lamuedra ordered the guards outside the door to remove his handcuffs.

"You're going to let him go home like nothing happened?" I asked Lamuedra.

"Not like nothing happened. He entered as an officer of the law and left as a civilian."

"But he left."

"It's a serious offense, and there's going to be a trial, but we don't have enough to justify detaining him right now. All in good time."

I took a deep breath and tried to calm down. I was surprised to find myself so outraged over Debarnot being let go, even temporarily. After all, I'd seen much worse cases where nobody ever went to jail.

◆ ◆ ◆

Fifteen minutes later, Echeverría stepped into Lamuedra's office. I'd called to bring her up to date, but she wanted to talk in person.

After Lamuedra finished telling her about Debarnot, the three of us fell silent for a while.

"I think he's telling the truth," I said eventually. "He liked the arrowheads, wanted to take them home, and had the bad luck of breaking the glass against the wall. Then he got paranoid and wanted to get rid of them. To cover his ass, he stole the fingerprints from my cabinet."

"If he's telling the truth, then whoever bought the arrowheads must be trying to complete the collection," said Lamuedra. "Which would be why they robbed the museum."

"That's what Alberto Castro thinks, too," said Echeverría. "We had breakfast at his hotel this morning."

"How's he doing?" I asked. "I was thinking about visiting him today or tomorrow."

"I'm sure he'd love that. He's fine, still a little shocked. And I think he blames himself a bit for not stopping the robbery."

"The last thing we'd have needed was some bookworm trying to be a hero," said Lamuedra. "If he'd tried to stop the attacker, we'd have ended up with two dead guys on our hands instead of one."

I agreed. Remembering Castro tied up in that cabinet gave me a pain in the stomach.

"Let's go over what happens next, then," I suggested. "Whoever attacked Castro needs two more arrowheads to complete the Panasiuk Collection: the one at Atardecer Ranch and the one in the safe at the courthouse."

"The first thing we should do is warn those people at the ranch to be very careful," said Echeverría.

"Manuel and I already warned them when we went down there," I said. "But I'll call and suggest again that they bring the arrowhead to the court so we can keep it in the safe."

"Good thinking. That's the best place for it. Estela and I are the only people in the world who know the combination."

Estela was the deputy judge who took Echeverría's place when she wasn't available. But she'd recently had a baby and hadn't set foot in the courthouse in months.

"Let's get back to Ortega's death for a second," Echeverría said. "Vera says he beat him to death in a fit of rage exacerbated by steroids. So, the motive was to settle a large gambling debt."

"And assuming Debarnot's not lying, now we know that Vera had nothing to do with the arrowheads disappearing," I added.

"Then we have two separate cases," concluded Lamuedra. "Ortega's murder and the arrowheads."

"Three separate cases," I corrected. "If we believe Debarnot, anyway. We've solved the homicide and the first robbery. But we still don't know who robbed the museum."

"Right," acknowledged Lamuedra. "And it's almost definitely the same person who bought the arrowheads off Debarnot. The physical description matches how Castro described his attacker: healthy build but not noticeably muscular, five foot eight, gray ski mask with black around the eyes."

CHAPTER 46

Echeverría drove me back to the courthouse, where I had parked, before going home. I was planning to do the same—I only went inside to drop off some paperwork—but once I was in the lab, I changed my mind and turned on the computer. I didn't have any particular task in mind, but I knew I couldn't just go home and stare at the wall.

While I waited for the computer to boot, I called Lali, the owner of Atardecer Ranch.

"The number you have dialed has been disconnected or is outside of the service area."

I remembered there wasn't much cell coverage at the ranch. Lali said it depended on the weather and where she was in the house. Sometimes they got a sliver of service, but usually they were totally cut off. Every day, usually in the morning, she climbed to the top of a hill to check her messages. I was calling at eleven at night.

I called again and got the same automated voice. I decided to leave a message.

"Hi, Lali, this is Laura Badía, from the court. Look, I don't want to scare you, but I think the chances of someone trying to steal the iridescent arrowhead you showed us are very, very high. Much higher than we thought the other day. So, please, sleep with one eye open and seriously consider bringing the arrowhead to town so we can protect it for a while. Like I said before, we have a safe at the courthouse. I promise we'll give it back as soon as we solve this case. This is just a measure to keep it—and the two of you—safe. Call me as soon as you get this. Thanks."

I hung up and stared at my phone. Had we done the right thing when we let her keep the arrowhead, knowing the danger she was in? A little voice in my head said that if something happened to her, or if something had already happened to her, it would be our fault.

My phone vibrating in my hands pulled me from these dark thoughts. The screen showed my aunt Susana's black-and-white profile picture from years ago: a strong young woman pointing her Browning at the camera.

"Hi, Aunt Susana," I said.

"Honey, it's me, your aunt Susana."

Her voice was trembling, like she had been crying.

"Yeah, I know. What's wrong?"

Silence.

"Aunt Susana?" I insisted, springing out of my chair.

Her voice was very different than usual. She spoke in a monotone, stumbling over her words. She was clearly reading from a script.

"Laura, if you want to see me alive again, bring the iridescent arrowhead to the willow trees on Route 3, before Caleta Olivia. Come alone at two in the morning. If you show up with anyone else, my death will be on your hands."

"Aunt Susana? Who's there? Are you okay?"

The line went dead, and I felt my legs turn to jelly. I had to grasp the table to keep from collapsing onto the floor.

CHAPTER 47

I paced around the lab, trying to think of what to do. The right thing would be to tell Lamuedra and Echeverría, since this was more than just a threat against my aunt, it was an extortion connected to the case we were investigating. At the police academy we had simulated plenty of kidnapping scenarios, but nothing, absolutely nothing, could have prepared me for a moment like this. Something inside of me, some kind of animal instinct, compelled me to protect my aunt's life at all costs. And if that meant going alone to meet with whoever the fuck had kidnapped her, that was what I would do.

My priorities were clear: I had to open the court safe and get the arrowhead. What wasn't so clear was how I would go about doing that, since only Echeverría and the deputy judge knew the combination. I looked at the clock. It was already eleven thirty, and the willows on Route 3 were a two-hour drive away. I had thirty minutes to get the arrowhead.

I called Echeverría, but she didn't pick up.

I called the deputy judge's number. While I waited for the line to connect, I thought about what I could possibly say to justify calling her in the middle of the night while she was on maternity leave. In the end I didn't need an excuse, since the line had been disconnected.

I felt like smashing my phone on the floor, but I managed to put it into my pocket. I continued pacing the lab, gliding my hand over the stainless steel table. After a few laps, I went upstairs to Echeverría's chambers.

As always, the door was unlocked. I lifted Echeverría's computer monitor and pawed around until I felt the metallic edge of a key. I'd seen her hide it there a thousand times.

"Let them find it," I'd heard her say on more than one occasion. "It's no good without the combination."

I went to the window and kneeled in front of the gray safe. I inserted the key and turned it, then pulled on the handle, hoping against hope that the last person to open the safe had forgotten to scramble the combination. The mechanism made an oily clicking sound and turned a little, but the solid door didn't budge.

I realized I didn't even know how many numbers were in the combination. Fortunately, the gold lettering on the dial indicated the make and model of the lock. The perfect question for Dr. Google.

The Sargent and Greenleaf 6739 combination lock is fitted with three wheels and can therefore be opened with a combination of three two-digit numbers between 01 and 99. To enter the combination, turn the dial fully at least four times counterclockwise before stopping at the first number in the combination; then turn the dial clockwise three times, stopping when the second number is beneath the indicator for the third time; turn the dial counterclockwise for two full turns, stopping at the third and final number in the combination.

I stopped reading when I got to the part about how there were a million possible combinations.

Think, Laura. If you were the judge, what combination would you choose? I remembered the comical painting with personified numbers at a bar. I'd always suspected that the combination was somehow hidden in the scene, and I'd overheard parts of a conversation between Echeverría and her deputy that seemed to suggest that, too.

But the characters at the bar were the numbers zero through nine, and I needed three two-digit numbers. And besides, what could an eight shooting tequila or a four dancing the cancan in fishnets have to do with opening the safe?

I tried several combinations based on contrived interpretations of the painting. When I ran out of ideas, I attempted more mundane solutions. I tried Echeverría's birthday, 03-22-62. Nothing. Then I looked up the deputy on Facebook, praying her privacy settings would let me see her birthday. 12-18-77. Nada. I tried reversing the numbers of both birthdays. Nope. Same with the date that they finished construction on the courthouse.

I put my ear against the cold metal and spun the dial, like I'd seen people do in the movies. I didn't know what I was listening for, but all I heard was the sound of the cylinder spinning on its oiled axis. I slammed my fist against the door, and my little finger got cut on the sharp edge of the tumbler. The only thing I'd managed to open was my skin.

I sucked on my wound, sat up, took a deep breath, and looked at the clock. To get there on time, I had to leave immediately. Gripped by a sense of powerlessness and unimaginable rage, I kicked the wheel as hard as I could. The safe didn't budge, but I did hear a loud *crack* from inside my shoe. I couldn't suppress a grunt of pain.

"Laura, what are you doing?" said Echeverría, behind me. Her voice was severe.

I turned around and saw her standing with her hands in the pockets of her gray suit. Her eyes were going back and forth between me and the key in the lock.

CHAPTER 48

"Why on earth are you trying to kick open the safe?"

"I had an idea," I stammered. Echeverría arched her eyebrows, waiting for me to make more sense. "I thought that we could make a plaster mold of the arrowhead."

I had no clue why I said that. It was the first thing that popped into my head.

"A mold? Why?"

"We could make a resin replica and put a GPS tracker in it. And then we could use the fake arrowhead as bait to find the rest of the collection."

"Put a GPS tracker in an arrowhead? Laura, you've been watching too many spy movies."

"No, it's not that absurd! They're making them really small these days," I said without the faintest idea of whether that was true or not.

"Not to mention that however good the resin is, it's not going to fool an expert collector."

"We only need them to believe it's real for a few minutes. I was looking online and found a special resin that imitates opal. They use it in jewelry a lot."

Another whopping lie. *Shit, shit, shit.* There was no way Echeverría was buying it.

"And this James Bond scheme of yours couldn't wait until tomorrow?"

"Oh, you know me, Echeverría. Anyway, I don't need to tell you how important this case is to me. Sorry for being a workaholic. I should follow your lead and never be at work after hours," I said, gesturing at the clock.

Echeverría chuckled. "Look, Laura, my situation is very different from yours. You're still young. You should make the most of these years. You'll end up regretting it if you spend all your time at work." She sighed heavily and leaned against her desk. "I learned that lesson too late, after I'd already lost everything. It's a long story and I don't usually tell it, but I think hearing it might do you good. Do you have time to hear the confessions of a defeated workaholic?"

No, I thought. There was nothing I wanted less at that moment than a long story.

"To tell you the truth, I'm a little pressed for time. Rain check?"

"Pressed for time? It's midnight."

"I want to get the arrowhead in the plaster as soon as possible so that first thing tomorrow we'll have the mold."

"Of course. And you thought kicking the safe would be the fastest way to open it."

I looked at the floor and put my hands behind my back, like a little girl being mocked at school.

"To be honest," I said quietly, "a while ago, I heard you and Estela talking about the safe and this painting. I was trying different combinations. I wanted to get the arrowhead tonight, to save time. I swear that I was going to tell you first thing tomorrow if I got it open."

She shook her head and sighed with an air of reproach. "When are you going to start doing things right, Badía?" she said, taking the painting off the wall. She turned the canvas around and pointed to one corner where a series of numbers was written in pencil. "Read them to me backward. I don't open it very often, so I don't know it by heart."

How did I not think to look on the other side? I thought, berating myself as Echeverría crouched in front of the lock.

"Zero, nine. Fifty-eight. Twenty-two," I said, mentally repeating the combination to commit it to memory.

She fiddled with the dial for a few seconds, then pulled hard on the small handle. The iron door opened, its thick hinges squeaking slightly.

"Here's the arrowhead that won't let you sleep, Badía. Do whatever it is you're doing with plaster, but then put the mold with the arrowhead back in to let it dry in the safe overnight, and close it. And know that we're calling a locksmith to change the combination tomorrow."

"Thank you, Your Honor."

Without a word, Echeverría closed the safe and left. I heard her go downstairs into the records office.

◆ ◆ ◆

I put the plastic box containing the arrowhead in the pocket of my windbreaker and ran to the lab, where I filled a plastic cup with plaster powder. Then I added water and stirred it as quickly as I could, getting little white drops on the table and my clothes in the process.

Once the paste was ready, I poured it into a plastic container the size of a cigarette box and put on the lid. I went back to Echeverría's chambers, put it in the safe, and closed the door.

I put my hand in my pocket and clutched the plastic box as I walked toward the exit. Echeverría was apparently still in the records office. When the police officer stationed just outside the building saw me approaching, he got out of his chair, unlocked the door, and opened it for me.

I stepped into the cold night and got into my Corsa. *Click* was the only sound it made when I turned the key. *Click* again. *Click, click, click.*

"Come on, not now. Don't do this now," I implored my car, but it didn't listen. I cursed everyone who had ever smilingly told me it was "just a matter of time" and got out, slamming the door behind me.

Both sides of the street were deserted. Then I heard the courthouse door open and saw the officer who had let me out approaching.

"Won't start?" he asked with the superheroic attitude so many men take when they encounter a woman with car troubles.

"It's the battery. It's been failing for a while."

"Ah, well, if you want, I can pull up my car and give you a jump."

"No, no, that's okay," I said, checking the time and seeing that I should have left twenty-five minutes ago.

"But look, it's no trouble—"

"No."

He held up his palms in pseudoapology. "Okay, it was just a suggestion."

"Sorry, I've been a little stressed the past few days," I said, putting a hand on one of his arms. "Can I ask you a huge favor?"

"Whatever you want."

"Can I borrow your car to go buy some cigarettes?"

"I didn't know you smoked."

"Only very occasionally." I smiled.

"Take it, no sweat," he said, digging in his pockets for his keys, which were attached to a Boca Juniors keychain. He handed them to me and pointed to the only car in the lot besides mine and Echeverría's. "It's the white Clio."

"Thank you so much. I'll be right back," I said.

"I'm not leaving here till seven. You can have it as long as you need."

I'll take you up on that, I thought. I smiled and trotted off to his Renault.

It started on the first try. When I looked at my phone to check the time, I saw that I had a voice mail. I played it as I slowly drove away from the courthouse.

"Hi, Laura, it's Lali, from Atardecer Ranch. I just got your message about the arrowhead, and there's no reason to worry. The archaeologist Alberto Castro was here yesterday, and he told me the same thing, that someone's trying to get the whole collection together and that we'd better keep it in your safe. He said he'd call and make arrangements to give it to you as soon as he got back to town. So, don't worry, it's safe. Maybe he held off calling because he got back late and didn't want to disturb you."

At last I understood everything. I slammed a fist against the steering wheel and floored the accelerator.

Lali was wrong. Castro had called me. But he had made my aunt do the talking.

CHAPTER 49

After an hour and fifteen minutes doing ninety, I saw the silhouette of the willows against the yellow glow of Caleta Olivia on the horizon. As I'd expected, there was no car in sight, just the willows and the small bridge over the dry riverbed.

I turned onto a narrow dirt road that connected the pavement to the riverbed. My headlights lit up the branches of a few more willows—there had never been more than ten—which grew flat and crooked, thanks to the wind and the endless drought. There was a car parked behind the largest one. After a moment, it flashed its headlights at me.

Alberto Castro stepped out, awkwardly brandishing a .22 pistol. He wasn't wearing a ski mask or trying to conceal his identity in any way. He walked around the car, opened the passenger-side door, and extended a hand to my aunt, who spent a few seconds debating whether to take it. After gallantly helping her out of the car, he pointed the gun at her, almost timidly. Reluctantly.

"Turn off the engine and your lights, and get out of the car," he yelled, narrowing his eyes, blinded by my headlights.

I did as he said.

The silence of the night was disturbed only by the swaying of the willows. I looked up and could barely see the cement beams holding up the bridge. To our right, the full moon outlined the undulating willows in silver.

Castro was standing a step behind Aunt Susana. He hadn't tied her hands or feet, but he was pointing the handgun between her kidneys.

"Put your gun on the ground," he shouted.

"What gun?"

"Put it on the ground," he insisted, pushing his gun deeper into my aunt's back. She closed her eyes and took a small step forward.

Castro's tone sent a chill through my body. There was a nervousness to his voice, like he didn't want to be doing what he was doing. Like he was straining to get through this and every minute hurt.

I reached under my windbreaker, drew my Browning from its holster, and pressed the release. The magazine fell to the ground. Then I pulled back the slide to eject the chambered round, which clinked against the rocks at my feet. I threw the now-harmless pistol to my right.

"Come here."

I took two steps toward him.

"Stop," he said when I was about fifteen feet away. "Toss me the arrowhead. And please, Laura, no tricks."

His last few words came out between short, sharp breaths, and I saw a silvery flash on his face. It was the moon, reflected in a tear that was rolling down his cheek, toward his white beard.

"Throw it now," he insisted. I did.

Castro caught the plastic box without ever taking his handgun off my aunt. Clutching the box between his pinky and ring finger, he took a small flashlight out of his pocket, turned it on, and put it in his mouth. He opened the box and verified that it was, in fact, the arrowhead.

"You can get in your niece's car, ma'am. I'm sorry for the unpleasantness."

He put the flashlight and arrowhead in the same pocket. My aunt took a timid step forward. Then a faster one, and then another, gaining speed until she was walking as fast as a seventy-three-year-old can over a rocky riverbed.

"Let's get out of here, Laura. This guy's nuts," she said when she reached me. She took a few more steps. Then she collapsed onto the ground.

CHAPTER 50

"Are you okay, ma'am?" Castro asked, gesturing for me not to move.

Aunt Susana didn't get up, but she did roll over and look at him, her eyes filled with hate. She had landed on her nose, which was now bleeding in fat, frequent drops. She got on all fours and crawled the remaining seven feet to the car. Leaning against the hood, she managed to stand, get inside, and close the door.

Castro lowered his gun and took two steps toward me. He had the pained, repentant look of a cornered man.

"Will you let me tell you why?" he said with a smile that didn't come close to disguising the anguish on his face.

"You don't have to. I already know. It's the most important arrow-head collection in the world."

He shook his head and tried to speak, but before he could, he was overcome by the same hoarse cough I'd heard the day we found him tied up in the cabinet.

"Wouldn't it have been better to put them in a museum rather than keep them all for yourself?"

"Keep them for my . . . why on earth would I want a collection of arrowheads? I can see any arrowhead, anywhere in the country, anytime I please."

"You mean you're going to sell them?"

Castro nodded, almost unwillingly. The sweat in the folds of his neck sparkled in the moonlight, like the tear had.

"I guess everyone has their price," I said.

"Yes, and two hundred and sixty-seven thousand dollars is well above mine."

"Well, that's a specific figure. I'm guessing you already have a buyer?"

"Something like that."

"Where's the collection?"

Castro lifted his face so he could look me in the eye, then shook his head. "I can't tell you that. You know I can't. I just torpedoed my career and my reputation for that damned collection." He let out a resigned chuckle when he heard his own words. "Maybe it's cursed after all."

"If you tell me where they are, I might be able to get them to reduce your jail time."

"I'm not going to serve any jail time, Laura."

His tone wasn't insolent. If anything, it was matter-of-fact. He was telling me a piece of information he was absolutely certain about.

"I don't get why you had to do all this. You're *the* authority in your field. You know more about Tehuelche archaeology than anyone else, anywhere. You travel around the world giving talks—"

"You have no idea what the world of research is like," he interrupted. "You have no idea. It took me thirty years to get where I am. Yes, I'm a chair at UBA, and yes, they invite me to give talks abroad. But I don't have a peso to show for it."

"Yeah, whatever. We're all hurting. Most of us manage to get by without robbing museums. There are lots of people worse off than a university professor who flies around the world talking about rocks."

Castro shook his head, grinning bitterly. "They can fly me to Venice or Las Vegas to give a presentation, but their 'honorariums' don't pay the bills."

"You must get a salary."

"Yes, a professor's salary, and for the past twenty years they've barely let me keep half of it. When I separated from my wife, I had to pay child support for Lautaro, our son, for fourteen years. The payments stopped when he turned eighteen, but the year after that he knocked up his girlfriend. Alicia was born six years ago, and five years ago my son was killed in a motorcycle accident."

He paused to take a breath. He closed his eyes tight.

"Alicia's mother declared herself insolvent and sued me for child support. When a child's father dies, if the mother cannot provide for the child, the grandfather, if he has no underage dependents of his own, is obligated to provide for the child financially. You work for a court. Did you know that was the law in this country? If I don't pay, I can't see the only granddaughter I have. The only grandchild I will ever have."

"And that justifies kidnapping an old woman and betraying a friend like Echeverría?"

"All Alicia's mother cares about is money. She leads a life that's well beyond her means, built on debt, credit cards, fees . . . and pills. Antidepressants, mainly. And she uses her daughter—my granddaughter!—as a bargaining chip. If I pay, I get to see her. If I don't, I don't."

"You didn't answer my questions."

"Laura, I could have just driven away. I want you to understand. It's important to me that you understand."

I said nothing, but I gave him the iciest stare I could manage.

"All I did was buy the arrowheads on the black market. For my work, I'm constantly monitoring online classifieds and illegal markets for archaeological material. And when I saw the ad for that collection, I made an offer on the condition that it be taken down immediately. I had to sell my car at a loss to pay the guy—it was a twenty-year-old Fiat Uno—but it was a bargain. With the right buyer, I knew I could sell the collection for a hundred times more, even with three of the pieces missing."

"So you came to Puerto Deseado to buy the arrowheads, pretending like you were helping us with the investigation."

"You have it backward, Laura. Echeverría called me and asked for help. For the past twenty years, I've been visiting Puerto Deseado every year or two for field studies and to do consultation work at the museum. I've known Echeverría since she was just starting out as a lawyer. When she saw this case involved lithic art, she invited me to come."

"And while you were 'helping' us with the case, you bought the arrowheads we were busting our asses trying to find. You bought them off a *cop*."

"When the seller who agreed to meet here turned out to be the pudgy police officer I'd seen guarding the courthouse, I couldn't believe my eyes."

At least Castro's story fit with what Debarnot had told us.

"Yeah, well, good thing you were careful and wore a ski mask. But you know what? I'm not interested in your story, because right now I have to take my aunt to the hospital to make sure she's okay."

"I treated her like a duchess."

"You kidnapped her and now she's bleeding, you son of a bitch! You could have sold the arrowheads you got from Debarnot and been done with it, but no, you couldn't resist completing the collection. How do you explain that one? Was it for more cash or out of some kind of weird archaeological fetish? You even told us someone had attacked you, just so you could steal an *additional* arrowhead from the museum. You want to tell me which employee you paid off to lock you in that cabinet?"

"I didn't have to pay anyone off. I'm the only culprit here. Those sheet metal cabinets have the locking mechanism exposed on the inside. If the key is in the door, you can turn it from within by pulling on the rods in the frame."

"Yeah, sure. And you tied your own hands and feet by yourself?"

"I did, Laura. There are dozens of amateur magicians explaining how to do things like that on YouTube."

I heard the Clio door open behind me.

"Laura, let's go," my aunt shouted.

I took a step back, staring at Castro with every ounce of hate in my body.

"Laura, I wish this could have ended differently. I think we would have been good friends in better circumstances. Have you forgotten about our trip to Calafate? All those talks we had?"

"No, I haven't forgotten about that time you pretended to be my friend so you could use me for information."

He looked down and his chest deflated, like he was very tired. "Laura, I wish you would understand me. I didn't have any other choice."

"What kind of bullshit is that? You robbed a museum, lied to me, and kidnapped my aunt, all out of greed. Tell me something, because it's something I never get with you people: What good is all that money going to do you, if the police are going to be chasing you all over the country?"

"I'll only have to hide out for a few months."

"Oh no, you'll have to hide out a lot longer than that. I am personally going to make sure that they find you. You will never be able to rest."

Castro looked straight at me, suddenly relaxing. It seemed like the gun was going to slip out of his hand. There was a look of harmony in his eyes, almost a look of peace.

"Just a few months, and I will rest," he insisted. "I'm sick, Laura. I am very sick. It wasn't the curves that made me vomit on our trip to the glacier. And it's not the cold southern climate that's given me this damned cough."

"Like hell."

"It's true. All of this is so I can leave something to Alicia. So when she turns eighteen, she can live a different life than her mother. Since I won't be there with her, I want her to get a good education, to be able to travel the world a little—"

"I don't want to hear another word," I said, and turned my back to him.

"Laura, don't leave."

I ignored him and continued walking.

"Laura, stop right there. I'm pointing the gun at you, Laura. Don't take one more step."

I walked faster, knowing he wouldn't shoot. He'd have to be a much rottener bastard to do that. There was warmth in his eyes, like there had been that day at the glacier. Something told me that he was telling the truth, that all these crimes were just the desperate actions of a cornered man.

If they were, I understood. And if he was lying, I'd make sure we caught him. But right then, I had to take my aunt to the hospital.

I wiped away a tear and looked at him one last time over my shoulder. He was still there, still pointing the gun at me. I think I might have seen him smile for an instant. I turned toward the car, where my aunt was waiting.

Then I heard a gunshot.

And another.

And another.

"Take that, motherfucker!" Aunt Susana shouted, her shoulder supported on the open car door. Her arms were out, and her hands clutched a weapon that I immediately recognized.

A quick scan of the ground confirmed my suspicion: the fall that gave her a bloody nose had been pure theatrics. My Browning wasn't where I'd dropped it. Neither was the magazine.

I turned toward Castro. He was propping himself against the fender of his car and staring down at his hands, which were trying to cover the holes in his gut. He looked up at me, bewildered, like he had just woken from a strange dream. Then he slowly slid down the car, eventually resting against one of the front tires.

"Aunt Susana, what did you do?"

"He was pointing his gun at you, Laura. That son of a bitch was going to shoot you. Let's go," she said, getting in the car.

I looked at her, worried. She was pale and gesturing for us to leave. But I ran to Castro as fast as my legs would take me.

"What are you doing?" I heard my aunt yell behind me.

Castro was holding his head up. His eyes were closed, and his mouth had curved into a smile that I thought looked calm. Blood was trickling out of the corner of his mouth, dyeing his beard red.

He made a guttural sound, and the smile became a grimace. He said something, but all I caught were a few vowel sounds. An *ah* and an *ee*.

"Don't talk," I said, calling an ambulance. "Help is coming."

When I finished talking to the dispatcher, Castro gestured with his head to the trunk of his car and tried to say that word again.

". . . *Icia* . . ." was all I understood.

"Alicia?" I asked, pointing to the trunk. "Alicia, your granddaughter?"

He nodded several times, and then the muscles in his face froze in a wince. He took two or three more breaths, then stopped trying to talk, then stopped moving altogether. I pressed two fingers to his wrist. No pulse.

I stood and walked to the back of the vehicle, pulled a sleeve over my hand to cover my fingertips, and pressed an oval button on the trunk. The trunk opened with a hydraulic buzz. It smelled like new carpet.

The interior lights came on, revealing a fraying, scuffed backpack. When I opened it, my mouth dried up instantly.

I'd never seen so many bundles of American dollars in one place.

CHAPTER 51

The backpack was extremely heavy. I pushed aside the cash at the top, revealing more underneath. There were at least twenty-five bundles of hundred-dollar bills. Over a quarter million dollars.

The rumble of a truck crossing the bridge above my head pulled me from my trance. If Castro had already sold the Panasiuk Collection, why had he risked trying to get the last arrowhead? How much more had they offered him for the missing piece? Could it have nothing to do with money? Maybe he suffered from some kind of professional obsessive-compulsive disorder and couldn't resist completing the collection.

"Are you okay, Laura?" Aunt Susana shouted.

"Yeah, I'm coming," I yelled back over the wind without taking my eyes off the backpack.

I took three deep breaths, trying to calm down and decide what to do. It was the most money I'd ever found at a crime scene. The few other times I'd found any significant amount of money—always far less than the sum in front of me—it ended up disappearing. I wondered who would end up with that fortune if I didn't take it myself. Commissioner Lamuedra? Someone even higher up the ladder?

I mentally converted the sum to pesos to get a better idea of how much was really in that backpack. Over four million. For a second, I fantasized about what a fortune like that could buy. A remote cabin somewhere in the mountains where there weren't tourists yet, for example. That would still leave me with plenty to open some kind of small business and start a life free from murderers, thieves, and the various other lowlifes I dealt with every day. Holding more money than I would earn in ten years—and more than I could save in forty—I realized that I was starting to get tired of the police force, the court, the morgue.

I reproached myself and clenched my teeth: *Finding money and being sick of your job have nothing to do with each other.* It wasn't my money, period. Not to mention it had come from the theft and sale of historic artifacts. It was illegal every way you looked at it. Touching that money would make what Debarnot did look like an innocent prank.

Before greed could get the better of me, I closed the trunk and ran back to my aunt. She was sitting sideways in the driver's seat, her feet sticking out the door.

"What were you doing?" she asked.

"Looking for a first aid kit."

"For him?"

"For you. For me. I don't know . . . I don't know, Aunt Susana."

"Is he dead?" she asked feebly.

"I think so."

Another truck crossed the bridge above us. We were silent until the sound of the engine faded in the distance.

"What did I do, Laura?" she asked, her hands rising to her face. "What did I do?"

I crouched down next to the open car door. My aunt's knees were on the same level as my head. I grabbed her and looked her in the eyes, which had gone glassy.

"It's all going to be okay, Aunt Susana, don't worry," I said.

Between gusts of wind, we heard the far-off sound of sirens.

"What are we going to say?"

"The truth. Castro was pointing his gun at me and you shot him. Both of our lives were in danger. It's all going to be okay, you'll see."

"Laura?"

"What is it?"

"I've never shot anyone in my life."

"This guy deserved it," I said to calm her down.

"He was pointing his gun at you."

"You did the right thing, Aunt Susana," I insisted, even though I was positive Castro didn't have the least intention of hurting us.

She didn't respond. Her eyes focused on an undefined point over my shoulder. She looked like a boxer who couldn't get up for another round. It was the first time I'd ever seen her defeated.

It had been a long fight for her, and she'd taken a lot more blows then she'd dealt, beginning when she was barely four years old. And now she was beside me, trying to steady her breathing and dry her tears with her fingertips. She opened her mouth to speak, but the words didn't come, and she again covered her face with her withered hands. The same hands that had made me thousands of breakfasts, the hands that had held me after my nightmares in the years after my parents' accident.

Her shoulders rose and fell as she was seized with an anguish I'd never seen in her, and I couldn't hold back my own tears. My aunt deserved better than the string of low blows she'd received almost her entire life. Much better.

The sound of the sirens was getting louder. The police and the ambulance couldn't be far.

Almost without thinking, I stood up and ran to Castro's car, carefully stepping around his body, which was still leaning against the front wheel. I opened the trunk, grabbed the backpack, and slung it over my shoulder. I heard the fabric tear, and a bundle of cash fell to my feet. The top flap had come unstitched, and green bills were sticking out.

I leaned over to pick up the bundle, only to have two more fall out. The blue police lights got close enough to illuminate the highest leaves of the willow trees. They couldn't be more than five hundred feet away.

I returned the two bundles to the backpack, held the top shut with one hand while supporting the bottom with the other, and hurried back to the Renault, where my aunt was waiting, and opened the trunk. I lifted the carpet, removed the jack and tools next to the spare tire, and put the backpack in the space where they'd been. Once the carpet was back in place, I put the jack and tools on top.

I shut the trunk, hearing the police pickup truck driving slowly over the gravel. The ambulance wouldn't be far behind.

I went back to Aunt Susana and gave her a hug. I tried to read her expression in the violet glow of the police lights, but I couldn't tell if she knew what her niece had just done.

CHAPTER 52

A few hours later, even from the warm comfort of Echeverría's chambers, the estuary looked foreboding. The falling tide was forcing the gray water toward the ocean, and the wind was rolling out threatening, white-crested waves.

"Come in, Badía. Sit down and tell me everything," Echeverría said, pointing to a chair across from her desk.

I gave her a lengthy explanation of what had transpired just a few hours earlier, acknowledging my lie to get her to open the safe and apologizing for not telling her Castro had kidnapped my aunt. I told the truth, broadly speaking, though I may have forgotten certain details concerning what happened under the willow trees. I especially may have forgotten about the backpack full of American dollars I'd hidden in my attic.

"So, Castro was trying to get the last arrowhead, even though he'd already sold the rest of the collection? That's a bit odd, isn't it? Wouldn't it have made more sense for him to get them all in one place before selling them?"

"Maybe he decided something was better than nothing? He could have arranged an extra fee with the buyer for the one we had, provided he could get his hands on it."

"I don't suppose he gave you any clues as to who that buyer might have been?"

"No."

"Or where the money from the sale might be? It wasn't in his car or in his hotel room at Los Barrancos. He didn't have time to hide it in Buenos Aires and then come back. And there's no way to deposit that much money at a bank without an explanation."

"Maybe he had another hotel room in Caleta Olivia or Comodoro Rivadavia? I doubt he was planning on coming back to Puerto Deseado after getting the last arrowhead."

"It's possible. Lamuedra's looking into it."

"What's going to happen to my aunt?"

"You don't need to worry about her. After she's discharged from the hospital, they'll take her to the station for testimony, and then she can go home."

"She won't be kept in custody?"

"No, not right now. There will have to be a trial, but she'll most likely be found innocent. Self-defense. In any case, even if she has to serve out a sentence, she'll get house arrest, since she's over seventy."

Echeverría looked at her ruby-red fingernails, lost in thought. It wasn't hard to guess what was on her mind.

"But *why*?" she finally asked. "I understand that simple avarice can drive people to terrible ends. We see that every day in our line of work. But something just doesn't fit. I would never have thought Castro was capable of something like this."

"You know better than anyone that when it comes to innocent or guilty, appearances can be deceiving."

She nodded, but she clearly wasn't convinced. I was about to tell her what Castro had said about being sick and having a granddaughter, but then I remembered Aunt Susana, who had the joys of due process to look forward to, in addition to being saddled with a guilty conscience for doing what she sincerely believed was the right thing. If she found out what Castro's true motives were, she would never forgive herself. Right then, sitting across from Echeverría, I resolved to take his last words to the grave.

There was an uncomfortable silence. At first, I thought it was because of what Echeverría had just said about house arrest, but then I realized it was because there was something important she hadn't yet mentioned.

"Laura . . . you know it breaks my heart to say what I'm about to say." She could have stopped there. I knew exactly what was coming.

"We're going to have to relieve you of your duties," she said. Her tone was severe, but she was avoiding eye contact. "You'll remain on the payroll, but I'm going to have to launch an inquiry because of all the irregularities. First it was the fingerprints, which were your responsibility, even though we know Debarnot stole them. Then there was the illegal collection of Vera's DNA sample, the lie you told me to open the safe, and the car you stole from the officer guarding the door. And, most critically, you went to see Castro alone instead of reporting your aunt's kidnapping."

"But Echeverría, what about the arrowheads? We still don't know who bought them off Castro."

"The Federal Police will take over the investigation. That transaction violated the Archaeological and Paleontological Heritage Protection Act. It's a federal crime, and we don't have jurisdiction," she said automatically, in a distant, professional tone.

"You can't take me off the case, Delia," I said, calling her by her first name for the first time in my life. "Are you really telling me you wouldn't have done the same thing?"

"What I would have done is irrelevant!" she shouted, slamming a fist on her desk. "No one gets to play the hero. I won't allow it. There are rules, procedures, protocols. And you, Laura, broke at least half a dozen of them."

She took a deep breath and tried to calm down before speaking again.

"I'm going to try to be as easy on you as possible," she said. "My guess is you'll be able to come back to work in six months. Maybe it's a blessing in disguise. You could go spend some time in the mountains. You're always saying how that's your dream."

"Six months?"

Delia Echeverría, the highest judicial authority in Puerto Deseado, shrugged. *Some things are out of my control,* her expression seemed to say.

CHAPTER 53

Five days after Castro's death, I went back to Echeverría's chambers. She had called me the night before and asked me to meet with her.

"How's your aunt doing?" she asked when I came in, rising from her chair to hug me.

"Hard to say. She's about as transparent as a brick wall when it comes to her feelings. I think she's just trying to get into some kind of routine."

"And how are you?"

"Bored. I can't get used to not working. But I have high hopes that'll be changing soon, since you were in such a hurry to meet with me."

She closed her eyes and shook her head. "I'm sorry, Laura, really, but there's nothing I can do. You know I'm the last person in town who can get away with bending the rules."

"What did you want to see me for, then?"

"Two things. First, I wanted to thank you for everything you did."

"Thank me? Delia, you suspended me."

"What the law says is one thing and what I think is another. And I think if you hadn't made life so difficult for Lamuedra and me, we would never have solved this case so quickly."

I let myself grin a little. "How's all that going, anyway? The case, I mean. Any word on Vera and Debarnot? Or Castro's buyer?"

"Well, Vera is still in detention. His lawyer ordered a blood test to determine his testosterone levels and demonstrate the use of steroids."

"But we arrested him two weeks after he attacked Ortega. A blood test now is irrelevant."

"Completely irrelevant. But saying he was under the influence of steroids and not wholly in control of his actions is the best argument they have. It'll be a simple murder trial. We'll see how many years he gets."

I looked out the window. A black cloud was moving across the estuary, heading straight for town.

"As for Debarnot, he's off the force."

"I can relate."

"No, Laura, you can't. *You* have been suspended, and sooner or later you'll be back. Debarnot has been permanently kicked off the force and will never again serve on any law enforcement body in Argentina. I wouldn't be surprised if he left town."

"What about the arrowheads?"

"That's the other thing I wanted to talk to you about." Echeverría smiled and lifted an index finger to indicate that I should wait a moment. She pressed a button on the landline on her desk. I heard the Harpy pick up on the other side of the door. "Isabel, tell him he can come in."

There were three knocks on the door, followed by the entrance of none other than the anachronistic Francisco Menéndez-Azcuénaga. In the hand that wasn't gripping his superfluous cane, he held what looked like an oversized box of chocolates. He handed it to me without a word.

"What is this?"

"Open it, Miss Badía."

I put the box on Echeverría's desk. It was made of wood, and the lid was affixed with three small golden hinges. I opened it, and a triangle of iridescent arrowheads filled the room with thousands of sparkles in every color of the rainbow.

Menéndez-Azcuénaga had added arrowheads eight and nine, completing the fourth line of the Fonseca Diagram. There was only one space missing, in the middle of the triangle, apparently intended for the last piece of the Panasiuk Collection.

"Wait . . . you were the one who gave Castro all that money for the arrowheads?"

"All what money?"

"Castro said he sold the arrowheads for two hundred and sixty-seven thousand dollars."

Teodor Panasiuk's grandson raised his eyebrows. "Indeed, if I had such a sum and were given the opportunity to purchase the arrowheads, I concede that I would have. But neither is the case. I've had nothing to do with any of this."

"It only took the feds three days to track down the buyer," Echeverría explained. "They called yesterday. It was some French businessman who apparently splits his time between Paris and Bariloche."

"How did they find him?"

"Castro's phone records. They said it was fairly easy."

She opened a desk drawer and handed me the plastic box Castro had caught before freeing my aunt. I opened it and palmed the arrowhead we'd found on the floor of Julio Ortega's house. It sparkled just as brightly as the other fourteen.

"What's going to happen to the collection?"

"It'll be put on display at the museum," Menéndez-Azcuénaga said.

"The owners of Atardecer Ranch have agreed to donate their piece," Echeverría added, pointing to the ninth arrowhead.

"Yeah? And what's Puerto Deseado's one-horse museum going to do to protect this million-dollar collection?"

She smiled before responding. "Mr. Menéndez-Azcuénaga here has generously agreed to buy a bulletproof-glass display case for the museum. It will be connected to a state-of-the-art security system."

"The people at the museum are so delighted that they've offered to name the main gallery after me," Menéndez-Azcuénaga said. "I've declined, naturally."

He reached into his pocket and pulled out a small tube of silicon glue, which he placed next to the collection. "Would you do us the honor of completing the Panasiuk Collection, Detective Badía? If it weren't for you, I don't believe we would ever have reunited all fifteen pieces."

"I would be honored," I said. "But first, can I ask you a favor, Mr. Menéndez-Azcuénaga?"

"Anything within my power, Miss Badía."

"Could you try to get the museum to change the name of the gallery?"

"I certainly could not. It is unnecessary, and it would be a scandalous act of vanity."

"I don't mean to your name."

"I beg your pardon?"

"I was wondering if they'd be able to change the name back to Patrick Gower."

"Who is that?"

"I'll tell you in a minute."

I placed the arrowhead in the empty space on the red velvet, completing the triangle.

After nearly three decades, the Panasiuk Collection was complete again. And for the first time in history, anyone who wanted to would be able to see it.

CHAPTER 54

I'd been prepared to offer more of an explanation when I took the backpack through airport security in Comodoro Rivadavia, but my badge and some court documents I'd printed at home were enough to placate the sleepy sub-officer running the X-ray machine, and I entered the terminal without answering a single question.

The flight to Buenos Aires took off on time and landed smoothly, neither of which is the norm. I kept the backpack between my feet the entire time and never got up to go to the bathroom. I'd periodically squeeze it between my ankles to make sure the bills were still there.

Unlike on previous trips, there was no friend waiting for me at the airport. I hadn't told anyone I was coming to town.

Two weeks had passed since the night beneath the willows. Echeverría had gotten Castro's body transferred to Buenos Aires on the province's medical plane two days after his death. According to her (we still talked sometimes, even though I wasn't working at the court), he was buried at a plot in the Chacarita Cemetery, next to his son. I wondered if Alicia had been at the funeral.

As for me, I couldn't get used to not working. I didn't know what I would do with myself for six months or for however long it took to clean up the mess I'd gotten myself into. Maybe a few days in Buenos

Aires would help me clear my head, though it wasn't exactly a vacation. If anything, it was a business trip.

I spent the night at a boutique hotel in Palermo, near all the embassies.

I was so nervous the next day that I could barely finish my coffee. In front of the full-length mirror in my room, I put on the blonde wig I'd bought in Comodoro Rivadavia and a pair of sunglasses that covered half my face.

I went out with the backpack slung over only one shoulder, clutching it under an arm. It was a damp, gray morning, and everyone was wearing long coats. I slowly walked the hundred feet between my hotel and the white building with palm trees across the street. I'd already scoped it out online.

I was stopped at the wrought iron gate by a tall, well-built guard wearing a white uniform that made him look like a sailor. He asked if I had an appointment. I said yes, and upon his request, I opened the backpack. He didn't even lift an eyebrow before waving me through with a slight bow.

The inside of the building was warm and dry, a welcome surprise in the middle of the Buenos Aires winter. A receptionist with her hair pulled back into an impossibly tight ponytail smiled at me with perfect teeth and asked how she could assist me. She had a Caribbean accent.

"They'll be right with you," she said after I explained why I was there. She typed something on her computer and gestured to a huge room with a white leather sofa. "You can wait in there."

I sat with the backpack on my lap. I again wondered if I was doing the right thing, and again decided that I was.

I leaned back on the sofa and took in my surroundings. The marble walls were decorated with oil paintings of exotic birds, idyllic beaches, and piers full of yachts. Hanging from the wall opposite me was a blue flag featuring a coat of arms and the Union Jack in the upper left-hand corner. Beneath the flag, gold lettering set in the marble read "Embassy of the Cayman Islands in the Argentine Republic."

It was less than five minutes before a man around my age with an enormous smile on his face came through one of the room's mahogany doors and shook my hand. He had an extremely fair complexion, light blue eyes, and very few hairs left on his head. He had a Caribbean accent, too, but unlike with the receptionist, you could tell Spanish wasn't his first language.

"Welcome, Miss Badía. My name is Gabriel Dawson," he said, gesturing for me to follow him through the door he had just come through.

We entered an office with modern white furniture. On each side of the room, there were two smaller offices with thick glass doors and walls. I could see trendy-looking desks in the two offices that didn't have their blinds drawn. Gabriel led me into one.

"So, over the phone you said you were interested in opening an account and making a deposit at one of the banks of the Cayman Islands. Is that correct?" he said, lowering the blinds so no one could see us.

"Yes, though there might be one small problem."

"What's that?"

I hesitated for an instant, trying to think how to explain myself.

"You needn't worry, everything we discuss here is strictly confidential. Not to mention you are now on Cayman soil. Our country's laws protect the identity of individuals who choose to bank with us. That's what makes us such an attractive destination."

"I can't declare the source of the funds."

He gave me an odd look. "If you could declare the source of the funds, why would you be banking in the Caymans?" he said with a grin.

He waited for me to smile back before he continued talking. "Many people choose to bank in our country precisely because we don't ask you to declare the source of your funds. And our government will never share information about account holders or balances, not even with the FBI or Interpol. What sort of sum are we discussing?"

"Two hundred and sixty-seven thousand dollars."

"There will be no problem, then," he said, opening a desk drawer.

He handed me a stack of brochures from different Cayman banks. I had never heard of most of them: Altajir Bank, Cayman National Bank, the CIBC FirstCaribbean International Bank, and so on.

"As I'm sure you'll understand, we are merely the consular representatives of the Cayman Islands in Argentina. We are not a bank. But, as finance is our largest industry, we facilitate the flow of capital into our country by opening an account at the institution of your choice and by making deposits on your behalf. As a free consular service, of course."

He then explained the advantages and disadvantages of all the banks, which had authorized the embassy to receive money and open accounts. I was amused to notice that even though his Spanish wasn't perfect, he knew the terminology of tax havens and capital flight better than I did, probably from repeating this explanation hundreds—if not thousands—of times.

All told, it was a perfectly legal, well-oiled offshore-banking machine.

"There is one catch, however," he said, after giving me a detailed explanation of each bank. "You would have a lot of explaining to do if you ever wished to transfer the money from the Caymans back into Argentina, or to any other country that isn't a tax haven. In practice, I would say it's impossible to do without raising red flags. So, if you wished to buy property, start a business, or otherwise use the funds all at once in Argentina, I'd have to advise you to bank elsewhere."

"But the money can be used in smaller amounts?"

"Yes, you will receive one credit card and one debit card, and you can withdraw up to five thousand dollars from any ATM in the world."

"Per month?"

He pressed his lips together, trying to stifle a smile. "Per day."

CHAPTER 55

"Javi, I waited for you here until I felt my heart break."

I stared at the sentence written on the green wooden bench before sitting down, trying to console myself with the thought that someone with a much bigger knot in their stomach had waited there before.

I checked the time. If I was lucky, the leaden-gray clouds would hold off for another fifteen minutes.

One by one, shiny new cars began parking on the cobblestone street that ran through the plaza. Two women greeted each other on the sidewalk, waiting in front of a manor house that had been built in an era when the cobblestone streets in the Caballito neighborhood weren't a relic of the past but an emblem of progress. A third woman joined the first two. They chatted, looked at their phones, and occasionally laughed.

Within five minutes, there were at least twenty more people waiting at the door. Almost all of them were women my age or maybe a few years older. I looked at each of them, wondering which was Alicia's mother. The blonde one with thick-rimmed glasses? The short-haired one with fake boobs? The one in yoga pants?

By the time they opened the double doors, nearly fifty people were waiting on the sidewalk. One by one, they went into the manor house.

Before the last parents got to go inside, the first were already coming back out, each accompanying a child in a white-and-gray uniform.

Most of the kids looked tired, saddled with brightly colored square backpacks that were larger than their backs. Some of them smiled while they talked to their respective grown-ups. Others were crying.

Alicia was one of the last kids to leave. It turned out her mom was the one with the short hair and fake boobs. I don't know why, but I'd had a hunch it was her. She was a little younger than me, and very pretty, but with a strange kind of beauty. Maybe it was because she'd plucked her eyebrows into two thin angles, which gave her a hard, almost wicked expression. Or maybe I just thought that because of what Castro had said about her.

Alicia had a subdued expression. She looked exhausted. I wondered if she'd had a particularly bad day. Maybe she'd gotten in a fight with a classmate or the teacher had yelled at her. Or maybe she'd been like that for two weeks, ever since someone—presumably her mother—told her that her grandpa had died.

Alicia said something and motioned with her hands. Her mom shook her head and pulled her by the arm. I recognized myself in the girl's sad face. And I recognized Aunt Susana, too, who had already been through hell by Alicia's age. At that moment, I hoped with all of my might that Castro had been wrong, that Alicia's mother was a capable and caring mother who would give her daughter a happy childhood.

I got up from the bench and walked away, wishing them the best and thinking about the alternative. What if the mother really was as superficial as Castro made her out to be? What good were Castro's plans then? Did it make any sense to leave money to a child raised by a terrible person? Had it been worth it for her grandfather to disgrace his name and taint his international reputation?

Would cash make Alicia's misfortunes any better? Only time would tell.

Eleven and a half years, to be precise.

That was how long it was until her eighteenth birthday, when she would receive a letter from the Cayman Islands stating that her grandfather had left her a bank account with two hundred and sixty-seven thousand dollars in it. Plus interest.

AUTHOR'S NOTE

Dear reader,

Thanks for reading this story! I hope you had fun with it. If you did, I'd love to hear what you think: cristian@cristianperfumo.com.

If this book left you wanting more, I'm sure you'll enjoy my other mystery novels and thrillers set in Patagonia:

The Sunken Secret (available in English and Spanish): An amateur diver risks his life searching for a ship lost in icy water.

Dónde enterré a Fabiana Orquera (available in Spanish and French): A journalist reopens an unsolved thirty-year-old murder case.

Cazador de farsantes (available in Spanish): A snarky skeptic spends his time exposing witch doctors, wizards, and other charlatans.

Finally, I'd like to invite you to sign up for my newsletter. That way, we'll be able to stay in touch and I can tell you whenever I publish a new story (and don't worry, I don't write very often and I never send spam). You can sign up at my website, www.cristianperfumo.com/en.

Till next time!

ACKNOWLEDGMENTS

This book wouldn't have been possible without huge help from my friend Celeste Cortés, a real-life forensic expert in Patagonia (and a far more professional one than Laura Badía).

I've also been lucky enough to consult with subject-matter experts who answered all my questions, even the most absurd ones. Esteban Byrne gave me an excellent introduction to the world of amateur bodybuilding. Alicia Castro answered many of my questions about Tehuelche lithic art. Mariano Rodríguez advised me on the Argentinian tax system. Hugo Giovannoni demystified the world of weapons and ballistics (and not for the first time). Many thanks to all of them.

I'd also like to thank Jorge Combina, one of the most talented Patagonian photographers I know, who gave me the rights to a gorgeous photo I've used for the cover of the first Spanish edition of this book.

The process of turning a manuscript into a book is a long one and requires many pairs of eyes. I'm grateful to the following people for reading the early versions of this story and for helping me make it better: Trini Segundo, Norberto Perfumo, Mónica García, Renzo

Giovannoni, Mónica Chrichton, Estela Lamas, Christine Douesnel, Lucas Rojas, Javier Debarnot, María José Serrano, Analía Vega, Ana Barreiro, Andrés Lomeña, Carlos Ferrari, and Lucía Distefano.

And, of course, I'm grateful to Trini, my partner in this life. Thank you for supporting me with this book, with all the previous books, and all the other craziness. It's easy to be happy when I'm with someone like you.

ABOUT THE AUTHOR

Photo © 2018 Goodnews

Cristian Perfumo lives in Spain and writes thrillers set in Patagonia, where he grew up. His first novel, *The Sunken Secret*, was inspired by a true story and has sold thousands of copies around the world. A successful self-published author, he has an established Kindle Direct Publishing following in Spanish-speaking countries. *The Arrow Collector* is his second novel published in English. Its original, Spanish version won the 2017 Amazon Annual Literary Award for Independent Spanish-Language Authors. Learn more about his work at www.cristianperfumo.com/en.